The
Malta
Conspiracy

Also by Frederic Mullally

Political
Death Pays a Dividend (with Fenner Brockway)
Fascism inside England

Novels
Danse Macabre
Man with Tin Trumpet
Split Scene
The Assassins
No Other Hunger
The Munich Involvement
Clancy

Diversions
The Prizewinner
The Penthouse Sexicon
Oh, Wicked Wanda!

The
Malta
Conspiracy

A Novel by

Frederic Mullally

Rupert Hart-Davis   London

Granada Publishing Limited
First published 1972 by Rupert Hart-Davis Ltd
3 Upper James Street, London W1R 4BP

Copyright © 1972 by Frederic Mullally

ISBN 0 246 10538 0

Printed in Great Britain by
Willmer Brothers Limited, Birkenhead

To my wife, Rosemary

The island of Malta provides the background to this novel and the place names used throughout are authentic. All of the characters in this work of fiction are, however, purely a product of the author's imagination and bear no resemblance whatsoever to any living person.

I

Sullivan heard her voice clearly as he came down the last few steps of St Christopher Street and out onto the broad carriageway of St Sebastian's Bastion. A young woman's voice. Tremulous. Close to panic.

'Leave me alone or I shall call the police!'

A Maltese accent? Possibly. He hadn't yet been long enough on the island to re-tune his ear to it. And he couldn't see her—only the backs of the two American sailors blocking her escape from the deadend tunnelway, or whatever it was cut into the stone building a few yards along to his right. The sun had just gone down, taking its long shadows with it, and the streetscape about Sullivan was held in a light dusk that seemed to empty the solid masonry of weight and substance, leaving it the two-dimensional fragility of a stage set. For populous Valletta, it was a curiously empty stage, even allowing for the district—an enclave of Government buildings—and the time

1

of day. Just Sullivan, two sailors and an invisible girl . . .

The big sailor, who was capless, raised a hand to his face and with brisk workmanlike movements flicked a cigar to the pavement and gave his pants a hitch from the waist. 'You'll have to shout mighty loud, honey. All the fuzz are up there in The Gut, tryin' to get between our boys and the Reds.'

The slim sailor let out a highpitched bitten-off laugh and began to advance crablike into the arched recess. 'C'mon doll! It'll only take you a coupla minutes and we'll see you safely outa here afterwards, me and my buddy— won't we, Al?'

'Sure will,' the big sailor said. 'Give you some dollars too, if that's what you want.'

'*Keep away from me!*'

Sullivan stepped forward, stopping a couple of paces behind the big American. He caught a glimpse of the trapped girl—dark hair over staring eyes; a yellow dress—as he called out, 'Carol! What the hell are you doing here?' Then his eyes went to the big fellow who had spun around—too damned nimbly, it occurred to Sullivan—and was sizing him up with a hostility at once mute and eloquent. From the corner of his eye he saw the slim sailor's head come around to stare at him. The girl was being dangerously slow on cue. He called out again, with a nice edge of irritation, 'Say goodbye to your friends, Carol, and let's go! They're all waiting for us up there!'

The big man said, 'What are you, Mac? You her husband or something?'

'That's right. Now, if you don't mind—' He walked straight past him, holding his hand out to the girl. It was a calculated risk but it was probably smarter, this way, than trying to talk their way out. As he turned back, the girl's hand in his, the slim American heeled around and laid his raised arms and head against the wall as if fighting nausea. *Overflow of adrenalin. He knows there's a fight sparking. Now it is up to the big bastard.*

The big bastard hadn't moved. There was a tight self-conscious grin on his broad face and his long arms were dangling. A Texan, by his accent. And by beef, too. Inches taller than Sullivan's six feet, and shoulders to match; but with a vulnerable-looking beer-belly.

2

With his right hand Sullivan passed the girl behind him, then pushed her through the gap between the sailor and the wall. Like that, his left was free to block and then hook to the belly till the right came back in play. He smelt the American's breath as he brushed past.

'Hey, what's the hurry? C'm back here!'

'Sorry ... Got a date with your commander. I'll give him your kindest regards Al.'

'Ya lyin' cocksucker!' It was bantering; good-humoured, almost. The danger was past.

He caught up with the girl and steered her left, up the stepped street.

'Fast as you can, without running.'

'My car—I left it parked by the bastion.'

'We'll get it later. Keep going.'

She had blue-grey eyes, carefully made up, in an otherwise unpainted face. Good cheekbones and a generous mouth. A straight finely-bridged nose and long dark hair with faint copper streaks in it. He would put her age at about twenty-two. He guided her to a corner table in the Blue Lounge of the Phoenicia Hotel. 'This lady,' he instructed the young bar-waiter, 'is in urgent need of a large brandy-sour. I shall have the same.'

She leaned back against the deep yellow cushions of the low sofa. The colour was back in her face, restoring its warm russet tan. She was as attractive a creature as any he had seen since flying into Malta two days earlier.

'I'm Bob Sullivan,' he said. 'Roving news-agency correspondent and spare-time Sir Galahad. Now it's your turn.'

'Daria Safad, citizen of the State of Israel. Agricultural exports department.' She smiled for the first time, and he thought, *Yes ... oh, yes ...*

'I wish,' she murmured, 'I could say I was a spare-time lady in distress, but one experience like that is going to have to last me a lifetime.' She gave a little shudder. *'Those animals!'*

'Every navy in the world has its share of them, Daria. They probably thought you were fair game, alone at this time of

3

night in that part of the town.' He hadn't framed it as a question. She could pick it up or let it lie.

She said, 'My office is in Old Bakery Street, higher up. I was working late on a report about—' she gave an amused little chuckle '—about the wine-drinking habits of the island. I'd been warned there might be trouble in Strait Street, and since I can never find anywhere to park in Old Bakery Street, I left the car on the bastion rather than on Palace Square, to avoid having to cross The Gut when I was finished.'

'Good thinking. I practically had to punch my own way out of it. If anyone was looking for a crash course in Russian and American expletives—' He leaned back shaking his head, as the waiter arrived with the drinks and deposited them with acolyte solemnity on the low oval table between their sofas. When the boy had withdrawn, Sullivan raised his glass in a toast. 'To a bumper harvest of Israeli lemons, or whatever it is you're pushing this year.'

'Wine, actually.' She smiled again, over the rim of her glass. 'And if my boss were to walk in now and find me drinking anything else—' She pulled a face before taking a sip at the brandy-sour. Behind Sullivan an exaggeratedly *pukkha* English woman's voice, loud enough to be heard in Poona, declared, 'Spitari's the real culprit! Unspeakable little man! High time we took over the island again.' Sullivan did not look around. Daria's eyes flicked in the direction of the voice, then back to him with a glint of amusement.

'Perhaps that wouldn't be such a bad idea,' she murmured.

He clicked his tongue, reproachfully. 'Spitari got in with a democratic vote, remember. On a neutralist platform. If Malta thinks the Soviet navy should be given equal facilities with the Sixth Fleet, then that's Malta's affair—for better or for worse.'

'That's not how we see it in my country. Spitari has handed our worst enemy—after the United Arab Republic—a staging-post in the Middle Sea they would never otherwise have had.' She put her glass down, then looked up at him frowning. 'I thought from your accent you were American.'

'It's what's left of the Irish in me,' he grinned. 'Plus the rub-

4

off from six years with an American wife. My passport says I'm British.'

'What do *you* say?'

'I say I'm a jet-propelled hobo. Home is where I unzip my typewriter. The world's my backyard. No national anthem goosepimples this skin.'

'Who pays you?'

'An international news-agency operating from Washington, London, Paris and Rome.'

'All Nato countries,' she observed, deadpan.

'The coincidence is political rather than journalistic. My stories earn roubles in Russia, pesos in Cuba and—' his grin broadened '—even the occasional Israeli pound, I believe.'

There were no sailors of either navy on Kingsway as he walked the Israeli girl back along Valletta's main street. Here and there, small groups of Maltese men and youths were engaged in fierce argument, and as they approached the Governor's Palace the debris of battle—broken bottles of Cisk Lager, Farson's Hop Leaf, dismembered bar-stools and trampled-on sailors' caps—marked how the running fight had erupted out of Strait Street and onto Palace Square where, earlier, Sullivan had watched the shore-patrols flail in with undiscriminating riot-sticks.

They crossed the square and turned down into Archbishop Street. 'Back at the London office, they'll be calling this "Sullivan's luck",' he chuckled, taking Daria's arm as they reached the intersection with The Gut. 'Out I fly on a completely different story—smack into history's first punch-up between the American and Russian navies.'

'What was the story you came for—or is that none of my business?'

'Little matter of a cargo of contraband cigarettes. Destination Sicily. I've got myself a berth on the boat that's running it.'

'Don't they know you're a reporter?'

'They know. I'm not naming names and I'm paying more for the sixty-mile trip to Sicily than it would cost first-class on the Queen Elizabeth to New York. The other thing is it's the skipper's last contraband run and I think he wants a good write-up to impress his grandchildren with in his declining years.'

Her car was parked a bare twenty yards from where she had been cornered by the sailors. While she found her keys and unlocked the door, Sullivan stepped to the wall of the bastion and stared out across the calm waters of Marsamxett Harbour, past Dragut Point, to where the great hulk of the *John F. Kennedy*, all garlanded with lights, stood out at sea, half-a-mile off the Sliema coast. He frowned, calculating the distance from the aircraft carrier to where, on the other side of the Valletta peninsula, a Soviet guided-missile cruiser, two Kotlin destroyers and a depot ship lay at moorings in Grand Harbour. The *John F. Kennedy* had been ordered to Malta by personal directive of the US President as soon as the news of the visit by the Soviet vessels reached the White House. It was a wilfully provocative move, in view of the fact that the Soviet navy had carefully scheduled its own maiden visit to avoid coinciding with units of the Sixth Fleet, and a less uptight US president might have thought twice about the wisdom of making it. But one could sympathise with his reaction. There had been a Nato HQ on Malta since as far back as 1953. Since then the Soviet naval presence in the Mediterranean had grown prodigiously. There was little the Americans or Nato could do, short of aggression, to change Paul Spitari's neutralist stance, but the Americans could at least see to it— if that was the way it had to be—that there was a US naval strike-force confronting a Soviet one at every move on the Mediterranean chessboard, including the vital Middle Sea. However, the risk the US President was taking—and this had been brutally rammed home by the battle in The Gut—was that the Maltese themselves might—

'Can I give you a lift anywhere?' Daria's voice, close behind him, broke into his thoughts and he turned around, smiling and shaking his head. 'Thanks, but I have an interview in five minutes with the Prime Minister—just along there at the Auberge d'Aragon. Matter of fact, I was on my way to check

6

its location when—' he chuckled '—when I heard you repelling these would-be boarders.'

She said, 'I haven't really thanked you for what you did.' She wasn't just being polite. There was sincerity in her voice, in the quiet regard of her wide unblinking eyes. She made no move when he encircled her lightly in his arms. 'I'll settle for a kiss,' he murmured, gathering her to him and gazing down into her upturned untroubled face.

'It's a small enough reward . . .'

As their mouths met her lips parted moistly and he could feel her hands on his back and the yielding up of her body to the embrace. This was no formal kiss for the victor : it was the stuff babies were made from.

He said, releasing her with reluctance, 'And dinner tomorrow night. Or am I straining my credit?'

'Not to breaking-point,' she smiled. 'I live off the coast road, just the other side of Paceville. The Villa Margarita. First dirt road after the new residential estate they're building on the left.'

'About eight?'

'Perfect.'

He waited until her car had rounded the bend of the bastion carriageway, then made his way up to the Auberge d'Aragon.

Paul Spitari—'that unspeakable little man'—was in fact a burly five-foot-ten with a thick mane of iron-grey hair and a voice gravelled by the long years of open-air speaking that had paved the way to his victories over, first, the Old Guard of the People's Party and then the ruling Nationalist Party itself. In Britain and in neighbouring Italy he was regarded—or had been until relatively recently—as a social-reformist in the old Labourite tradition—a Maltese Clement Attlee; a Saragat perhaps. To the Catholic Church in Malta he was a subversive, dangerously-unpredictable radical. To the island's organised working-class, to the anti-clerical element among the students and the intelligentsia, Spitari was the new broom that would sweep clean the ingrained dust of generations of paternalism, economic *laissez-faire* and political nepotism. He

7

was fifty-two, a grandfather twice over and—so it was said—
a poet of some distinction in the Maltese language.

He received Sullivan in an open inner courtyard of the
Auberge d'Aragon, its high walls garlanded with flowering
bougainvillaea, its centre-piece a stone fountain featuring a
chipped dolphin from whose gaping mouth a thin dribble of
water lamented four centuries of incompetent plumbing. He
did not budge from his cushioned cane chair but extended an
arm to accept Sullivan's handshake, at the same time nodding
dismissal of the young male secretary who had escorted
Sullivan through the corridors of the auberge.

'Forgive me, Mr Sullivan . . . I've had enough of that office
of mine for one day. It's cooler out here, and the stars make
soothing company.'

'I'm grateful you've spared me the time, Mr Prime
Minister.' Sullivan lowered himself into the chair facing
Spitari. 'Particularly after this evening's little eruption up
there in The Gut.'

'Ah, yes . . . that . . .' Spitari leaned back, tilting his face
skywards. 'I'm waiting just now for the Police Commissioner's
report. A bad business, my friend. The repercussions could
be—' he raised a weary hand and let it flop limply across his
broad chest. 'But that was not what you wanted to see me
about, Mr Sullivan—unless you were being clairvoyant when
you phoned my secretary this morning?'

Sullivan shook his head, grinning. 'Matter of fact, one of the
questions I wanted to put to you was why you allowed the
American carrier in at this time. The question's even more
pertinent now—wouldn't you agree, Prime Minister?'

Spitari nodded, slowly. 'My position hasn't changed, Mr
Sullivan. The election was largely fought on this issue—
whether Malta should become a member of Nato or take a
strictly neutralist stance between the two power-blocs. The
electorate made their decision, and you will recall my
ultimatum to the Nato powers on assuming office: either the
Soviet Mediterranean fleet was to be afforded the same
facilities as the Sixth Fleet and its Nato allies or else both
super-powers would have to stay away from Malta.'

8

'I recall it all right,' Sullivan chuckled. 'It swept one of my best stories off the front pages.'

'And it nearly swept *me* into Marsamxett Harbour. My opponents here thought I was just shadow-boxing during the election campaign. When the ultimatum was announced they came at me like a pack of wolves. The Nationalists screamed for a referendum. My own party was split right down the middle. The *Times of Malta* wanted me impeached. The Archbishop ordered special prayers to be said for divine intervention.' Spitari lowered his head to smile at Sullivan. 'You know who saved me?'

He knew well enough, but he shook his head. You did not make friends by robbing people of their punch-lines.

'The British Government. One day my own people are screaming for my head on a plate. Next day, the British prime minister threatens to cancel the balance of aid due to Malta unless I toe the Nato line—and overnight I'm a national hero! You realize, Mr Sullivan, we Maltese have become a very touchy people since we won our independence. For centuries, under successive foreign rulers, we lived by the principle: if you can't bite the hand that holds you down, you should learn to kiss it. Now we have all those years of subservience to make up for. *Nobody* is going to push us around and we don't need anybody's charity, particularly if it has political strings to it!'

'So that was when you tore up the defence agreement with the UK and gave the green light to the Russian Navy?'

'Right. And invited a resident Soviet ambassador. And exchanged trade missions.'

'Tell me something, Mr Prime Minister. What happens to Malta if war should break out between America and Russia?'

'In the past,' Spitari answered, 'only one thing was certain. As a staging-post for the Sixth Fleet, this little island would have been wiped out immediately by a Russian nuclear submarine or guided-missile ship. We have no antimissile defences. Now—' he shrugged his shoulders, 'with both fleets sharing our harbours the likelihood is that they'd have to settle for hitting each other with conventional weapons.' He let out a dry chuckle. 'I'd personally settle for turning Strait Street over to them—together with an endless supply of empty beer bottles.' Catching a signal from his secretary, who had reappeared under the arched entrance to the courtyard, Spitari started to push himself up out of the chair. Sullivan got in one last question as they walked together back into the main building.

'Are you taking any special measures, Prime Minister, to avoid a replay of tonight's schemozzle?'

'That won't be necessary. Neither side wanted this to happen, I feel sure. They'll make their own arrangements to prevent a replay, as you put it.'

He found John Carona in his office at the *Malta Mail,* proof-reading an editorial going into the next morning's issue of the paper. Sullivan had first met his Maltese friend back in 1964 when he flew to Malta to cover the Independence Day ceremonies. Carona had then been the *Mail*'s chief political correspondent. Elevated to Editor four years later, the pocket-sized newsman had swung a hitherto 'independent' *Mail* vigorously behind Spitari during the struggle for leadership inside the People's Party and the subsequent general election. It had cost the paper perhaps a quarter of its over-30s readership and a sizeable slice of advertising revenue; but with Spitari's electoral victory three months back, the *Mail* had come up smelling of violets and was now way ahead of the competition, with John Carona's voice—after Spitari's and the Archbishop's—possibly the third most influential on the island. He put down the galley-proof and got up from his desk as Sullivan walked in. His lean pointed features ('hawk-like' or 'vulpine', depending on the beholder's bias) wore the dark tan of a dedicated weekend sailor.

'Been expecting you for the past hour or so, Bob. You want us to book a call to London, or are you telexing your story?'

'I'll phone it, John, if there's a line going in about twenty minutes. I needed a few quotes from the PM.' He crossed to the desk his friend had cleared for him in a corner of the room and helped himself to some copy-paper from one of the drawers. 'What's new on the Battle of Strait Street?'

'The men are all back in their ships and neither embassy is making any comment till they get the commanders' reports— maybe tomorrow.'

'Have your lads found out yet how it got started?'

Carona tilted his chin upwards in the Maltese gesture of negation. 'How do any of these Strait Street brawls get going? One sailor starts making up to another sailor's whore in a bar. Or maybe he knocks over a fellow's drink by accident. Somebody starts swinging a fist and before you can say "Madonna!" the fight's spread to every bar along The Gut.' He picked up the galley-proof of his editorial and ran his eye down it, frowning. 'Earlier this week,' he muttered, 'the *Mail* was handing a bouquet to the Soviet Navy for the good behaviour of its men ashore. It's true, Bob ...' he looked up challengingly. 'A lot of Maltese people really had the jitters about this Russian visit. They'd been brainwashed into believing the Russians were some kind of sub-human atheistic savages. They got the surprise of their lives when those fellows came ashore—clean, blue-eyed, friendly; smiling at the girls along Kingsway without ever bothering them, spending their money in our shops, quietly touring our museums and churches.' He gave a little chuckle. 'Even the *Times of Malta* found a good word to say for them. "Their conduct," it allowed, "certainly compares favourably with that of other periodical visitors to our shores"—which was a pretty obvious crack at the Americans. You know what they're saying now, out there along Kingsway?'

'Tell me.'

'They're saying it was definitely the Yanks who started the trouble tonight. Next thing, they'll be chalking slogans up on the walls—"Yanks Stay Out!" and so on.'

'What's the answer, John? Alternate days shore-leave for the two sides?'

Carona shrugged. 'I put that to the Russian naval attaché, half-an-hour ago. He said he didn't think his people would suggest it. Personally, my guess is they're out to make all the public-relations capital they can from this, and any other punch-ups they can blame on the Americans. They're pretty confident their lads have the better discipline ashore.'

'They certainly have better means of enforcing it,' Sullivan grunted, sitting down at the desk and pulling the typewriter into place. 'Now, you get on with editing your parish broadsheet while I take care of the world's press.' He looked quickly over his shoulder, grinning broadly. He had suddenly remembered Spitari's comment on the 'touchiness' of his people.

Across the room, Carona was giving him the old 'up yours' sign.

The clock behind the hall-porter's desk at the Phoenicia Hotel was showing 10.55 pm.

'Gentleman waiting to see you, sir,' the hall-porter said, handing Sullivan his room-key. 'In there.' He nodded towards the central lounge.

There was a sprinkling of people sitting around. Only one of them was on his own: a redheaded youth in jeans and T-shirt. He got up as Sullivan strode over.

'Mr Sullivan? I'm from Peter Lund.'

'About the trip?'

'Right.' The accent was North of England—Lancashire, by that vowel-sound. 'We're shoving off in two hours' time.'

'Two *hours*? Hell—I understood it would be two *days*!'

'Something's come up. Mr Lund says you can have your money back if you don't want to come along. Otherwise, I'm to wait and drive you to the police to get your documents cleared.'

There wasn't much to deliberate. If the trip went according to plan he would be back in Malta in time for breakfast. All he was losing was a night's sleep. He said, 'Hang on while I go up and change.'

'Oh, and the skipper asked me to tell you we won't be putting back to Malta, this trip.'

Sullivan's eyebrows went up.

'He says he'll try to put you ashore somewhere along the coast of Sicily after we've unloaded the stuff, but if anything goes wrong we'll be heading back for Tunis.'

12

This was something else again. Another twenty-four hours, maybe, before he could get a plane back—longer, possibly. He thought quickly. Carona could telex the agency a follow-up story to the Strait Street brawl, if anything developed to-morrow. He would surely be back in Malta the day after that, even if they had to make for Tunis. Remembering his dinner-date with Daria, his mouth tightened over a silent 'Damn!' He would have to get a message to her through John.

'Give me about twenty minutes,' he said. 'I'll meet you in the Pegasus Bar—just along the corridor there, to the left.'

Upstairs, he tossed his shaving-tackle, passport, credit cards and travellers' cheques into a grip, together with a change of socks, underwear and shirt. He was pulling a roll-top sweater over a pair of jeans by the time the operator got Carona on the line. Sullivan briefed him on the change of plans and asked him to call Daria at her Valletta office in the morning.

'Fast work, Bob ... That bird's had more propositions put to her since she arrived than Malta has churches.'

'How many has she bought, would you say?'

'None—from any of the fellows I know, anyway. So of course she's been written off as a lesbian.'

'The fellows must be either naive or dead unadventurous. Anyway, thanks for everything, John, and I'll call you soon as I get back.'

The redheaded crewman was draining a pint tankard of Hopleaf when Sullivan joined him at the Pegasus Bar.

'Another pint, er—?'

'We'd better keep moving.' The young man put the tankard down and turned a solemn bony face to Sullivan. 'You can call me Stan,' he said. 'It's agreed with the skipper that you're not going to mention any of the crew by name in your write-up.' He was staring straight at Sullivan, asking for confirmation.

'That makes sense, Stan. I take it you're staying in the game after Lund quits?'

'Let's say that's strictly my business, shall we?'

The Gurkha was made fast to a rusty old scrapped barge on the south-east quay of the Marsa docks. She was a seventy-two-foot converted motor-torpedo-boat of the 'Dark' class,

13

fitted with two 2500-hp Napier Deltic 18-cylinder diesels giving her a cruising range of 1,500 miles and a top speed of 52 knots. She might just about be some rich eccentric's idea of a fun boat to keep in the Mediterranean, provided he didn't expect the Customs police to share his sense of humour. Certainly the boat's owner, Peter Lund, nurtured no such illusions. He picked up his contraband in one part of the Mediterranean and landed it in another, invariably at night. But in three years of running contraband across the Middle Sea he had never tried to smuggle so much as a bottle of duty-free whisky onto Malta. This the police knew, and so long as he kept it that way they had no reason to deny him the traditional hospitality of Malta's harbouring and repairing facilities. Besides, in order to help him respect the rules his cargo hatch was sealed by Customs as soon as he put into Malta and a night-and-day Customs guard placed on the boat (at Lund's expense) until he left Maltese waters.

The skipper was on deck, watching three of his Spanish hands making everything fast on deck, when Stan's car drew up at the quayside. He nodded a greeting as Sullivan crossed the iron deck of the barge to board *The Gurkha*.

'Sorry about this, chum,' he called out. 'Unforeseen complications.' He was a stocky Channel Islander with a greying beard close-trimmed about his copper-hued face. He had bought the Panama-registered boat and taken to full-time smuggling after his two bars in Tangier had been closed down by the Moroccan police in their crack-down on the Hippie drug traffic. He operated as a freelance—one of the last remaining owner-skippers not contracted to the Mafia-controlled smuggling ring.

Sullivan followed him into the saloon that had been built behind the small open bridge, to which it was connected by a short flight of steps. As he dumped his grip into a corner, Lund opened the grog-locker and took out a bottle of armagnac.

'We've time for a shot before we cast off.' He scooped up a glass and thrust it at Sullivan. 'I take it—' he gestured towards the grip '—you're coming along with us.'

'Looks like it—*whoa, there!*' Sullivan jerked the rim of his

14

glass up to cut off the flow of old armagnac from the tilted bottle. 'But what's this about not putting back to Malta afterwards?'

'Not convenient,' Lund grunted, tossing back his drink and then frowning hard at the bottle in his right hand, as if it were somehow a contributing party to the inconvenience. 'I'll refund whatever it costs you to get back.'

He had no chance to question Lund more closely until they were lying off the coast of Sicily, a couple of hours later, watching the approach of what they hoped was the Italian pick-up vessel on *The Gurkha*'s radar screen.

'If anyone had told me,' the skipper muttered, scowling up at the bridge where Stan was standing by the wheel, 'I'd be sitting out here under a last-quarter bleedin' moon with twelve hundred cases of cigarettes in the hold, I'd have told 'em they were out of their Chinese minds.' He reached for the armagnac bottle and recharged his glass, swaying gracefully with the swell of the sea under *The Gurkha*'s hull. 'When we radioed the lads in Syracuse for a rendezvous tonight they damn near blew their tops.' He let out a chuckle. 'Didn't take 'em long to get a pick-up organised, though, when I told 'em it was tonight or never.'

'Don't you usually land the stuff on shore yourself, Peter. Isn't that what those Zodiac rubber dinghies are for up on deck?'

'Sure. But it costs me ten dollars a case in bribes to the Eye-tie cops that way. I wanted to save the "extras" on this run, seeing as it's my last.'

'What are they sending out, Peter—a miniature submarine?'

'Nothing so sophisticated. Just a common or garden dredger.'

'A *what*?'

Lund was grinning broadly. 'They're bright lads, our Eye-tie friends. Seems this dredger's been dumping a couple of loads of shit out at sea every night for about a week now. The patrol boats have lost interest in the operation. Tonight the dredger's steaming out another mile or so to rendezvous with us. Ought to be a piece of cake.'

'All the same,' Sullivan said, staring into his glass, 'I'd have felt a lot safer covering this lark on a moonless night, as originally planned.' Without looking up, he added: 'What went wrong, Peter? I'll keep it out of the story, if that's what you want.'

Lund took another look at the radar screen, then moved to the companionway to peer up at the bridge.

'Keeping a sharp eye out, lad? They've no radar on that tub.'

'Aye, Skip. I'll sing out soon as I spot her.'

'They're good lads,' Lund grunted, turning back into the saloon. 'No complaints from *them* about doing the run tonight.'

'I'm not complaining, Peter—just curious.'

'As well you might be,' Lund nodded. He stood scratching his beard for a while; then, with a short laugh and a shake of the head, reached for the bottle and tilted it briefly over Sullivan's glass and his own. 'Might as well tell you the story. I doubt if you'll want to use it, but I can't see it doing me any harm anyway, since I shan't be putting back to Malta again—'cept maybe on some luxury cruise liner.' He sank into his chair and hunched forward, staring into his glass. 'It started the night before last with a Malt called Burgo who hangs around the Good Fellowship Bar at Marsa most evenings. This type buys me a drink or two and then he asks me if I'd like to earn a fast five thousand dollars for myself, with seven grand more to split among my boys. Nothing to do with contraband. No risks. All over in twenty-four hours. "Sounds too good to be true," I says. "Where's the catch?" He didn't want to talk there in the bar so I took him aboard the boat and after a bit of shilly-shallying he came right out with it, sitting in that chair where you're sitting now ... He wanted three of my crew—the fairhaired ones—to go ashore dressed up in Russian naval uniform.'

Sullivan remained outwardly calm, waiting for it. It wasn't easy. Every nerve of intuition developed over ten years of stalking the Big Story was flexing and twitching away like a dowser's hazel.

16

'This Burgo geezer would put half the money down at once and provide the uniforms. The lads wouldn't have to wear them for more than a couple of hours, he said. Then straight back to the boat to collect the rest of their pay-out. Real piece of cake he made it sound like.'

'What did they have to do, Peter? Desecrate St John's Co-cathedral? Piss into the Blue Grotto?'

'Nothing so public as that, mate. Like he said—there were no risks to this caper. Police protection even—in the person of a certain Detective-Inspector Avanzo, who was in on the operation and would cover my boys in the event of a slip-up.'

'Go on,' Sullivan said quietly.

'Well, the long and the short of it was that my lads were to go after dark to a certain spot just outside St Julian's and wait there, rigged in their Russian uniforms, till some Maltese girl came walking by—'

'*Any* Maltese girl?'

'Some unsuspecting sitting-duck Burgo was going to set up. Soon as she came by, the boys were to—' Lund broke off as Stan's head appeared in the companionway.

'Dredger just flashed us, Skipper. About quarter-of-a-mile off the starboard bow.'

Lund was up on his feet before Stan had finished.

'Right! Slow ahead, both. I'll be out in a jiffy.' He swung around to Sullivan as Stan's head disappeared. 'You'd better stay here till I give you the ok. Don't want you on the bridge till we're coming alongside.'

'Just a second, Peter. Last line to the Burgo story—what did the boys have to do to earn their wages?'

'Oh, that—.' Lund had plucked an electric torch from the chart-table and was testing the beam on the cabin floor. 'There was the rub, mate. They had to gang-rape the girl and beat her up a bit, betweenwhiles.' He stuck the torch into his belt and flashed Sullivan a piratical smile. 'I never even consulted 'em. The bastards would probably have done it for straight beer-money.'

'So you turned Burgo down—and that's why you got your marching orders?'

17

'Detective-Inspector Avanzo in person. Yesterday. "Get the boat out!" he said. "Within twelve hours." '

'And never come back no more?'

'Oh, no, he was smarter than that. The boat might be allowed back some time—after the skipper had proved he knew how to keep his trap shut.'

As Lund climbed up to the bridge Sullivan moved to the starboard window and peered across the slow-heaving sea, his eyes scanning the dark horizon for the darker silhouette of the dredger while his mind grappled with the implications of what he had just heard. The gang-raping of a Maltese girl by foreign sailors—be they Russian, American or British—would just about blow the island's top. It wasn't easy to think of any other single violation of Maltese hospitality that would more outrage and unite this nation against the culprits and everyone else who sailed under the same flag. Peter Lund's refusal to lend his men to this nasty plot did him credit. And it gave rise to two immediate and interlocked questions: Would that be the end of the affair? Who or what was behind it?

Burgo—whoever he was—should have done his homework a little more diligently before approaching Lund. This would have taught him that five thousand dollars was no great bait to an operator who could make £21,000 profit out of one night's run from Malta to Sicily. It might also have taught him that Peter Lund had been irrationally but virulently anti-American since the day, eight years back, he had been conned out of his life-savings by a Californian unit-trust 'expert' operating from Tangier. Burgo had goofed; but the precipitate expulsion of *The Gurkha*, coupled with the warning to Lund from a highly-placed Maltese cop, seemed to suggest that the rape plot was still held to be viable. But by whom? Was it possible the US Central Intelligence Agency could be a party to such villainy? Sullivan's mouth curled tightly at the corners. If the CIA happened *not* to be involved it was certainly not because they had no stomach for the operation. An outfit that dealt in murder and could be blandly unsqueamish about torture would hardly flinch from the 'constructive' rape of one Maltese girl. Still, the CIA was nothing if not painstakingly meticulous in the screening of its

18

would-be pawns and it seemed inconceivable that one of its agents would make such a direct and incautious approach, even to a professional lawbreaker like Peter Lund. The Nationalist Party opposition to Prime Minister Spitari, then? Certainly they would gain powerfully from any flare-up of public hostility towards the Soviet Navy; but—well—this just wasn't on. The party's leader, Doctor Enzo di Domenico—a devout Catholic with irreproachable personal standards of decency—was in complete paternalistic control of the party organization and the kind of person who would surely sacrifice political power for the rest of his life rather than connive at the rape of one of his countrywomen. It left the possibility that Burgo and his cronies were freelance *provocateurs* who had come to an arrangement with the CIA on a payment-by-results basis. If the thing came off, they would be in clover: if it failed there would be no egg left on the face of the CIA.

Sullivan's musings ended abruptly as *The Gurkha*'s engines changed pitch and the saloon floor tilted slightly over the thrust of its propellers. They were moving a little faster forward now and as he adjusted his balance the outline of the Sicilian dredger, softly illuminated amidships, came clearly into view. She was now about half a cable off, still to starboard and with her propellers barely turning over. Sullivan turned from the window to peer up at the bridge. Peter Lund, with one hand on the wheel, was pointing his torch straight at the dredger and, as Sullivan watched, the beam flashed twice, then twice again.

'All right for me to come up, Peter?'

'Stay where you are!' Lund had stuffed the torch back into his belt and, without taking his eyes off the dredger, was beginning to open up the throttles. He called sharply to Stan, who was watching the dredger through binoculars.

'Don't like the smell of it! They're supposed to answer that one!'

Stan's voice came over the throb of the engines. 'Let's take a look around her, Skip!'

Lund grunted and increased throttle, at the same time correcting course to keep well away from the dredger as *The Gurkha* made its sweep. They were about level with the

19

stern of the Italian vessel and just going into a wide 180-degrees turn to come around it when there was a sudden roar of engines from the trawler's concealed port side and a long low silhouette shot across the Italian's bows and snaked around, parallel with *The Gurkha*'s wake. The bright shaft of a searchlight split the dark sky, then swung and contracted into a blinding single eye, lighting up the saloon and bridge and forcing Sullivan to duck involuntarily sideways out of its silver glare.

2

'*Down, everyone!*'

Lund's bellow came a split second before *The Gurkha*'s engines roared into full throttle. There was an agonising pause while the powerful screws seemed to bite on air; then the floor under Sullivan gave a crazy tilt backwards as he let himself go at the knees.

He heard the gunboat's siren—strident, peremptory—then Stan's voice shouting something indistinct. There was an explosion of glass splinters from one of the cabin windows, and as the m-t-b went into a series of slalom swoops everything still loose in the cabin, including the armagnac bottle, seemed to hit Sullivan not once but again and again, vindictively. There was a rip of bullets through the cabin superstructure and a *zing* of lead ricochetting off the bridge's armour-plating. *Let's hope that little lot didn't have Peter Lund's name on it.* It hadn't. A final sharp swerve from course pitched Sullivan the

21

width of the saloon. Then *The Gurkha*'s hull rose gradually up out of the rushing sea and she was planing on the surface, sweet and true.

He sat up, kneading a shoulder that felt it had been clouted by one of Mayor Daley's public servants. There was a scurry of feet along the port deck, an excitement of voices from the bridge, and then Lund was peering down into the saloon, his head and shoulders softly silhouetted by the gunboat's waning searchlight.

'You all right, mate?'

'Great—apart from five fractured ribs and a dislocated shoulder. Have we lost the fuzz?'

'Eye-tie bastards, foxing our radar like that!' Lund took a long look astern, then came on down into the saloon. 'They're not all ponces, I suppose. If the master of that dredger hadn't tipped us off by ignoring our signal, they'd have done us for sure this time.'

'Smart helmsmanship, Peter, that's what got us away.'

'Helmsmanship, my arse. The bloody boat was out of control half the time, what with engines full out and me dodging the Eye-tie bullets.'

'What happens now?'

'Full steam for Tunisia. I'll have to sort things out with the boys after we get there. Maybe try another run before new moon.' He flashed his torch around the cabin floor, grunted, and made for the grog-locker. 'Sorry you didn't get your story, chum, but as my old man used to say, "Man proposes, God forecloses".'

'I got a story all right. The Italian papers'll lap it up. What I'm concerned about now is how long I have to hang around Tunis waiting for a flight to Malta. What's the private charter situation?'

'Not too rosy, now this new colonel's taken over.' Lund had found a bottle and two glasses. He carried them to the chart table and switched the light on. 'I might be able to get you on a boat. Here—knock this back.'

Sullivan stopped the glass, halfway to his lips. He was staring at Lund's left thigh. 'Don't look now, Peter, but I think you've been hit.'

22

'Eh? Now don't play silly—' Lund, following Sullivan's gaze, was staring down at the glistening patch spreading around the rip in his faded Levis. He put his fingertips gingerly to the patch and brought them away, red-tipped.

'*Blood*,' he whispered, looking up. And Sullivan, seeing the skipper's eyes roll white, dropped his drink just in time to catch the doughty smuggler as he slumped forward in a dead faint.

He spent the whole of the next day in Tunis, profitlessly in quest of a private plane to fly him to Malta. But late in the evening, in the bar of the Hilton Hotel, he met the captain of the yacht *Felice Sirena*, bound for Malta on the return leg of an Eastern Mediterranean cruise. The yacht was under charter to a Stockholm businessman and his family. Sullivan presented himself aboard after breakfast the next morning, explained his problem, and was cordially invited to join the Swedes on the yacht's home run.

Dusk was beginning to gather, thirty-six hours later, as the *Felice Sirena* put into her berth at the Ta'Xbiex marina. Sullivan grabbed the first cab cruising along the front and ten minutes later was at the desk of the Phoenicia Hotel requesting his key. The hall-porter had to ask him twice, with an intermediate cough, for his room number before Sullivan heard what he was saying. His eyes were fixed on a copy of *The Times of Malta* lying beside the bellpush. His mouth had all of a sudden gone dry.

'Can I have this paper?'

'Of course, sir. Your room number, please?'

He read the headlines and the introductory paragraph on his way up in the lift.

MALTESE GIRL'S TERRIBLE ORDEAL

SAVAGE RAPE BY RED SAILORS

MAJOR CRISIS IN MALTA—USSR RELATIONS

An eighteen-year-old girl from Spinola Bay, Miss Lina Mazzi, was last night being given medical attention at St Luke's Hospital after being assaulted and raped, she alleges, by three Soviet naval ratings while on her way to visit friends in Is-Swiegi. The police have taken a full statement from the victim and an interim report has been rushed to the Prime Minister ...

There was something unreal about the whole thing. It was like having a dream about a dream. In his room, Sullivan dropped his canvas grip to the floor, sat down on the edge of the bed and read on.

In a statement issued just before *The Times of Malta* went to press earlier this morning, the police described Lina Mazzi as an attractive young lady from a respectable working-class family whose breadwinner, Mr Charles Mazzi, a former fitter with the Royal Engineers, died when she was fifteen. Since then, Lina has lived with her mother, Mrs Mary Mazzi, and three younger brothers at 44, Cyclops Street, Spinola Bay. She left school at sixteen to take a job as room-maid at the Europa Hotel.

The girl's nightmarish ordeal began, it seems, when she was passing one of the many new building developments overlooking St George's Bay at approximately nine-thirty yesterday evening. Two Soviet sailors, one of whom spoke a few words of broken English, hailed her and, gesticulating towards a half-completed villa, gave her to understand that one of their comrades had come to grief inside the house.

The trusting girl, wishing to be of some help, followed the Russian sailors into the villa, whereupon she was seized and gagged by all three men and certain articles of her clothing forcibly removed. She was then brutally violated by all three men in turn. Her struggles and pitiful pleas for mercy were answered with curses and blows.

Finally, as she lay half-conscious on the floor of the back room where the assaults took place, one of the sailors unfastened the crucifix Lina always wore on a gold chain around her neck and clipped it back after manipulating the cross with his fingers, while the others

looked on laughing. Later, Lina found that the sacred
cross had been twisted into the symbol of the communist
hammer-and-sickle. . .

After the Soviet sailors had fled, Lina managed to
stagger as far as the coast road near St Andrew's Barracks where a passing motorist—an English resident of
Madliena—took her in his car to St Julian's Police
Station.

Up to the time of going to press, no arrests had been
made and an 'Iron Curtain' of silence had been rung
down at the Soviet Embassy. The Prime Minister, Mr
Paul Spitari, was withholding comment 'until further
information became available'. However, Dr Enzo di
Domenico, leader of the Nationalist Party, spoke for all
Maltese and civilized people everywhere in a midnight
statement to *The Times of Malta*.

'There can be no peace of mind for the people of this
island,' he declared, 'until the barbarians who have
perpetrated this hideous crime are securely behind bars
and the nation that spawned these evil monsters is out-
lawed from our society and our shores.'

Sullivan put the newspaper aside and sat staring into space
for a long minute. Then he reached for the bedside telephone
and asked to be connected with John Carona at the *Malta
Mail*.

'Bob! Your office has been driving us crazy here! Where the
hell have you been, man?'

'That can keep. What have you given them so far on the
rape story?'

'Everything we know. I just telexed them about the
cancellation of Soviet shore-leave and today's mass demonstrations outside their embassy. They're screaming for an interview with the girl and one with Spitari. You coming over?'

'Be with you in five minutes. Thanks, pal, for covering for
me.'

He finished buttoning a clean shirt and combing his damp
hair in the taxi as it sped around the bus terminal and in under
the Victory Arch into the capital. His mind had been roller-

coasting since he had slammed down the telephone and headed for a cold shower. There might be about one chance in a thousand the 'Soviet' rapists were the real thing: he had to allow for that chance and play his moves carefully or he might—just might—be off on the wildest goosechase of his career. By now, every TV and news-agency team based on Rome would have a man or men heading for Malta or already on the island—and any hopes of getting a beat on them through an interview with the ravished girl had been blown somewhere out at sea, on the sundeck of the *Felice Sirena.* He had only two leads to work on for the moment; the man Burgo, who had made the approach to Peter Lund, and Detective-Inspector Avanzo. But if he alerted Avanzo at this stage, he would risk finding himself on the first plane out of Luqa Airport, with a police escort all the way across the tarmac. And if, to secure himself against this contingency, he sought the influential protection of John Carona by telling him what he knew, he could kiss goodbye to the Big Story; no editor worth tuppence-worth of printer's ink would elbow his own newspaper out of a world-beat on a story like this.

There was another hang-up. Just supposing that, even without Carona's help and complicity, he was able to establish the girl Lina had been raped by bogus 'Soviet' sailors directly or indirectly in the pay of the CIA? Was he, Sullivan, prepared to have this appalling story splashed across the world's press and TV screens? The repercussions it would have on the United States' presence in the Mediterranean hardly bore thinking about. The depth of America's moral nosedive would be matched only by the boost to Russia's image and credibility. Well, he could start worrying about that if and when the story looked like being wrapped up. Meantime he would get on with his job, which was to rake mud in search of the truth, regardless of who got splashed in the process . . .

John Carona's desk was a mess, with sheaves of telex interlapping galley-proofs, photographic prints and all the accumulating bumph of a meglomaniac newspaper editor incapable of delegation. He was on the telephone, cadenz-ing away in fluent Italian, as Sullivan came through the door, and he nodded as the Irishman headed straight for the desk and

26

plucked up a glossy print at random. The nod clearly said, 'That's the girl.'

She had a sexy-looking young face, with wide eyes and ripe lips, and though her thighs were a bit on the fleshy side her torso made anatomical music inside the modest onepiece swimsuit. She was smiling into the camera and shading her eyes from the sun with one hand.

He picked up a pink sheet of paper with the typed heading, 'Medical Report', scanned it and put it down with a grimace.

'That's the picture the foreign press is going for,' Carona said, hanging up the telephone. 'One of our lads got it out of her mother this afternoon and we've been flogging the prints like crazy.'

'I'm overjoyed for you, John. Can you brief me on what's been happening?'

'Well, let's see what you ought to know ... Lina's been discharged from hospital but the Soviet commander is refusing identification parades for her and the cops aboard his ships. Nothing unexpected in that ... Still no statement from Spitari, except a visit to the girl in hospital this morning and a plea to us editors to try and keep our cool till the police have produced their report.'

'Are you playing ball?'

'*I* am, and I'm going to lose sales over it. The competition's pulling out every stop. I hear *The Times of Malta* is giving up the whole of its front page to a statement by the Archbishop instructing parish priests throughout the island to agitate from their pulpits this Sunday for an immediate suspension of diplomatic relations with the USSR ... What else, now? Oh yes—I just had a call from the Secretary of the General Workers' union. Buddy of mine. He wanted to know why Spitari hasn't yet issued a formal denunciamento to the Russians. Give him a chance, I said. He summoned their Ambassador to the Auberge d'Aragon at midday. Now he's obviously waiting for the police report. Not good enough, my friends says. Unless the Prime Minister takes some kind of positive action immediately, the GWU is coming out on a token strike.'

'And that's the PM's own union—right?'

'Right.'

'How do you rate my chances of getting to see Spitari this evening?'

'Pretty dismal. He won't even talk to me. But he's giving a press conference tomorrow morning at ten.'

'And the girl?'

Carona gave a shrug. 'She's been at police head-quarters all day, except for a trip to the scene of the crime. I wish you luck, but—'

'I'll be back to file copy in about an hour. Can you book me a call to London for, say—' he checked his watch '—about ten pm?'

'Will do. Sure I can't sell you a picture?'

'Yep—when you've got something the other boys haven't had. Ciao, John!'

He took a cab to Police Headquarters in Floriana, a few minutes inland from Valletta, and told the driver to wait. The police constable standing by the main entrance moved to block his passage into the forecourt of the building.

'Yes sir?'

'I'd like to have a word with the officer in charge of the Lina Mazzi case.' He took out his international press-card and held it before the policeman's incurious eyes.

'Sorry, sir. No press inquiries before eleven o'clock tomorrow morning.'

'What do you mean, no inquiries before tomorrow morning? I'm making one right now, aren't I?'

'You may be making one—' the constable looked away from him, colouring '—but you won't get any answers. And you won't get in there,' he added, jerking his head backwards.

'Will you do one small thing for me then? Will you take a message to Detective-Inspector Avanzo?'

'Not possible, sir.'

'Why not? He *is* the officer in charge of the case, isn't he?'

'That's correct. But his instructions are to keep the press out of headquarters today, so you're just wasting your time here.'

I wouldn't exactly say that, Sullivan smiled to himself as he crossed the road to the parked taxi. It made for a certain lightening of spirit when one's first dart went straight into Double Top. The game was off to a good start . . .

There was a small door in the wall, about fifty yards along from the main entrance to Police HQ and it opened as Sullivan's taxi drew level with it and a girl in a white frock stepped onto the pavement. He caught one glimpse of her and called to the cab-driver to stop. She was halfway across the road, heading for her parked car, when he shouted her name. She paused, peered back at him through the dim street lighting, then let out a sharp exclamation. The fact that her hand went straight to her hair, Sullivan took to be a sign he was not yet relegated to the Third Division. He caught up with her and they crossed the road together.

'I'm sorry about our dinner-date, Daria. You got the message from Carona?'

'It was very thoughtful of you. So I kept yesterday evening free for you—and spent it watching some very bad TV.'

They were standing by her car. There was reproach in her tilted chin and forced-away eyes, but no anger. He said, 'I was then about a hundred miles out at sea. The smuggler ran into a trap and we had to *imshi* for Tunisia.'

'How interesting. You must tell me about it, some time.'

She was lovelier even than the memory-pictures he had summoned up on that shake-down bed in the saloon of the *Felice Sirena*. He wanted to get in the car with her now and drive across the island to some candlelit restaurant terrace overlooking St Paul's Bay. But he had another call to make and then a story to file.

'Could we meet later, about ten-thirty?'

She shook her head. 'I'm on my way to a dinner engagement.' She was staring across the road at the police building. 'They've already made me late in there, going on about my work-permit.'

'Tomorrow evening, then? I'll call for you at eight, laden with gold, frankincense and myrrh.'

'You mustn't,' she smiled, 'think you can corrupt a nice Jewish girl with mythical Christian handouts. Just bring me a big fat order for Israeli wines. We give a discount for quantity.'

29

He told the cab-driver to stop fifty yards short of the Good Fellowship Bar on the Marsa quayside. He got out and, ruffling his hair as he went, walked the rest of the way, brushed aside the bead curtain over the entrance and advanced stifflegged and slightly off-course towards the bar at the far end of the narrow, harshly-lit room. There were mean little plastic-top tables along the walls on either side, and two of them had been joined together for a card game involving four silent players who gave him a bare glance as he went by. Behind the bar a short flight of stone steps ended at a cramped landing where someone with his back to the bar was speaking quietly into a telephone. The barman, who was completely bald, removed the cigar from his mouth to give Sullivan his undivided attention.

'Greetings, my friend,' said Sullivan. 'And may the blessings of the Almighty be on this enchantin' esh-establishment.'

The barman nodded warily.

'I come in peace, for nourishment and information. But first, my good landlord, the nourishment. A large and undiluted scotch, if it please ye.'

The barman served him the drink and stood watching as Sullivan raised the glass, sniffed sensuously at it, took a tentative sip and stared up at the ceiling for a long moment.

'It's all right, sir?'

'The barley,' Sullivan intoned quietly, 'would appear to be from MacIver's farm in Auchtermuchty, five harvests back . . . The maize? Ah, the maize . . .' He lowered his head to gaze fixedly at the barman. 'I could be wrong 'bout the maize. No-one's infallible—barrin' The Holy Father, of course.'

'Have a guess, sir,' the barman prompted.

Sullivan took another sip, rolling the liquor around his mouth and closing his eyes as he swallowed it. 'With qualifications,' he said at last, 'with minor qualifications, I rest my reputash'n on the assersh'n that the maize in this rather trite and prosy blend was cut just south of latitude fifty-eight, at no great distance from Portahomack in the county of Ross and Cromarty . . . But enough of that. Could you be telling me, good mine host, where I might find a vessel known as *The*

Gurkha—the same being owned and mastered by one Peter Lund?'

'*Gurkha?*' the barman frowned at the man who had descended the steps while Sullivan was speaking and was now standing at the bar a few paces away from him. 'I think she's left, hasn't she?'

The man nodded but looked away, avoiding Sullivan's eyes. He was about forty, with the torso of a tall man reduced to medium height by the wrong size of legs. He had thick black sideburns and wore a heavy gold signet ring on the second finger of his right hand.

Sullivan said, 'Could you oblige me, sir, by tellin' me when she's expected back. I had an appointment today with her master.'

'Can't help you.' The man drained his glass, put it down and started to button up his jacket. 'Ciao, Tony,' he nodded to the barman. 'I'll see you later.' And with another nod for Sullivan, he turned and stalked out onto the quayside.

The barman pulled an apologetic face. 'He's not to know, you see. You might be anyone—know what I mean?'

'Look—' Sullivan shook his head in well-simulated bewilderment. 'I'm an engineer looking for a job. I know what this fellow Lund does with his bloody boat. No secret, is it?'

'Well, you see, he wasn't to know that—'

'Who do you mean— "He"?' Sullivan cut in peevishly.

'That chap—Alfonso Burgo. Have another word with him later, or tomorrow evening about this time. Him and Captain Lund were having a drink together here, only a few days ago.' Tony the barman gave Sullivan a fat wink. 'He knows all right. Just being, you know, careful.'

'I am greatly obliged to you, sir,' Sullivan said, detaching a Maltese pound note from the roll in his trouser pocket and laying it to rest on the marble-topped bar. 'Have a large drink with me, my friend. And my blessing on you and yours.' He raised one hand, pontifically, then turned slowly around and set an unsteady course for the doorway, pausing to bow gravely to the cardplayers on his way out.

So far, so good. He had satisfied himself that Detective

31

Inspector Avanzo and the gentleman called Alfonso Burgo were no figments of Peter Lund's imagination. And he had done this, he hoped, without alerting either of them. The next step would be to establish, if he could, some direct link between Burgo and the CIA on the one hand and Burgo and Lina Mazzi on the other; and of these two undertakings the second offered not only the better prospect of success but also—in the light of Lund's story—a piece of vital circumstantial evidence that the 'Russian' gang-rape had in fact been a put-up job.

On his way to the taxi, he stopped under a street light and took another look at *The Times of Malta*'s page-one story. There it was: '44, Cyclops Street, Spinola Bay.' He checked his watch. The time was nine-thirtyfive.

'How long will it take us,' he asked the cab-driver, 'to get to Spinola Bay?'

'*Spi*nola Bay?' the driver corrected his faulty stress. 'About a quarter of an hour, sir.'

'Let's go.'

The call to London would have to wait. Bill Topper, back on the Mediterranean desk, would know from John Carona that he was back in Malta and would assume that if he was late filing copy or making any contact with the office it was because he was out—as usual—chasing the story behind the story. In any case, what else of any hard news interest could he file that night that hadn't already been fed to the world's press, without alerting the competition—not to mention Burgo & Company—to the line of sleuthing on which he was embarked? He would talk to Bill Topper from the hotel, as soon as he got back. He would give him a hint of the story he was after and suggest he move another agency man to Malta at once to cover day-to-day developments in the situation, leaving Sullivan free to burrow away into its murkier depths.

Again he asked himself, as the taxi sped around Msida Creek, if he wasn't digging for a barrel-load of high explosive it might be more prudent to leave safely buried. Supposing it had been an undercover British outfit that had plotted and executed this unsavoury deceit: would he still go full-out for an exposure, well aware of the appalling damage it would do to Anglo-Maltese relations? Or again: supposing it had been an American newsman to whom Peter Lund had told his story: would the American have gone straight to work on it, or dropped it like a hot potato? The answer to that last hypothesis, anyway, was immediate and comforting. Sullivan had only to think of the top-ranking American journalists he had so often worked with, inside their own country and abroad, to know beyond doubt they would have gone right on digging, whatever the consequences. 'Patriotism' came in a hundred shapes, including Samuel Johnson's 'last refuge of a scoundrel' and Spiro Agnew's litanies of hate. There was only one shape to Truth: it was made up of all the ascertainable facts; and the honest journalist's first duty was to dig them out.

The taxi was labouring now up a steep and narrow road overlooking Spinola Bay. It took a sharp turn right and came to a stop halfway down an even narrower street of terraced houses.

'Number forty-four, sir,' the driver said, pointing. 'If you want me to wait, I'll have to park further up, where the road is wider.'

'I'll meet you up there, then.'

The street-door of Number 44 was already open, and as he stepped over the threshold he heard English-speaking voices coming from a room off to the right. There was a sudden silence, then the flash of a camera-bulb. Sullivan stopped at the doorway to the room, taking in the scene with a tight smile.

A short fat woman dressed in funeral black was perched on the edge of a sofa with a silver-framed photograph clutched in one hand while the other dabbed a white lace handkerchief to her nose. Behind the sofa, solemn and bespectacled, stood a youth of about sixteen. As the photographer crouched for another picture, a tall, sandy-haired man wearing a khaki bush-shirt with bulging pockets turned, following the youth's distracted glance, and showed his teeth in a huge grin.

'Bob, you old bastard! Nobody told me *you* were on this caper!'

'You astonish me, Ed. I left standing instructions your office should be informed of my every move. Why aren't you in Cambodia?'

'Don't be like that, pal. Where I *should* be is in Tel Aviv —except they took me off the plane when I landed there yesterday and shoved me on the next plane to Rome to cover this story. Where you staying?'

'The Phoenicia. This lady, I take it, is Lina's mother?'

'Right. Help yourself. I'm through soon as we've got the pictures.'

'Plenty of time . . . Which hotel are you at, Ed?'

'The Hilton, down the road. The office has some kind of deal with them, worldwide. I'll buy you a drink there when you're through.'

Sullivan nodded. He was a good operator, Ed Summers— one of UPI's best roving correspondents. It wouldn't do any harm to get his personal slant on the story . . . He moved into a corner of the small room, with its dark, diligently polished furniture and museum-like arrangement of Victorian gewgaws and gaudy religiana, and waited as the freelance photographer packed up his equipment and Ed Summers took sympathetic leave of Mrs Mazzi and her eldest son. When they had gone he introduced himself to the woman and took a seat facing her.

'How is your daughter, Mrs Mazzi?'

'She all right. Maybe coming home tonight.'

The youth, who had taken his place beside the mother, leaned forward, eager to help. 'My mother is not very good at English. She says that Lina is all right and maybe she will be coming home tonight.'

Solemnly, Sullivan thanked the lad for his deft interpretation. 'Would you ask your mother if there is any possibility of my being able to talk to Lina when she gets back home?'

Mrs Mazzi dabbed at her nose and said, 'Not possible. Policeman come with her and stay here. Inspector tell me she must not talk with men from newspapers.'

'I'm afraid it will not be possible,' the youth explained. 'There will be a police guard here to stop the press from talking to my sister.'

'By order of Inspector Avanzo?'

'Yes.'

'She says, "Yes".'

'I see.' Sullivan decided to short-circuit protocol and address

34

himself directly to the lad. 'There's something that puzzles me . . . Wasn't it rather late in the evening for a young Maltese girl like your sister to be out visiting friends, that distance from home?'

'Yes, yes!' the youth nodded rapidly, then fell silent, waiting on Sullivan's next question.

'She go after finish work, from hotel,' Mrs Mazzi supplied. 'She work late that week. From back way she leave. Up—' she waved her handkerchief aloft '—up by new houses to road on top.'

'My mother says that she was—'

'Thanks, son, I got the gist of that. Whom was she visiting—does either of you know that?'

'Friends,' they declared simultaneously.

'Anyone you know?'

The lad shook his head.

'Never tells me!' the mother cried aloud, suddenly and violently enough to make Sullivan jump. 'Never, never! My husband dead! If he not dead—*aaa-ee, Madonna!*' She slumped sobbing across the arm of the sofa.

'One last question,' Sullivan said quietly to the boy, 'and then I'll stop bothering you. Does the name Alfonso Burgo mean anything to you?'

'Burgo? I know many Burgos.'

'Alfonso Burgo?'

'No, sir. I never heard of that one.'

He was not lying. Murmuring his thanks to the two of them, Sullivan got up and went out to find his taxi.

They were stopped from entering the air-conditioned bar of the Hilton. 'You have to be wearing a tie, sir,' said the watchdog guarding the entrance.

Sullivan peered into the dimly-lit interior. 'I see two men in there,' he growled. 'One is a Mafioso, the other a notorious child-murderer, But they're all right, I suppose, on account of that thin strip of cloth dangling from their collars?'

The watchdog looked distressed. 'If you'd like to speak to the manager, sir—'

'Come on,' Ed Summers chuckled. 'let's sweat it out on the terrace. You can jump in the pool between drinks.'

'Without a tie on?'

They orderd a bottle of champagne and turned their chairs to face the dark seascape. Over to the right, beyond St Julian's Point, the *John F. Kennedy*, 'dressed over all' sat brooding like some monstrous armour-plated hen. Sullivan switched his gaze towards the invisible horizon and wondered if Peter Lund were somewhere out there beyond, waiting for a signal from his Italian colleagues.

Summers said, 'You been thinking what I've been thinking, Bob?'

'About what?'

'The rape story. It smells to high heaven.'

'Two doctors have confirmed the girl was banged dizzy.' He was deliberately misinterpreting Summers' remark. 'They put in three stitches where the zip of one of their pants tore what I believe is known as the outer labia.'

'I don't mean that. She got the treatment all right. But I'll lay odds it wasn't from Russian sailors. In *uniform*, yet? And that story of the twisted crucifix!' Summers shook his head. 'Too much, man!'

'Why should the girl lie about it, Ed?'

'That's what I'm going to find out. Maybe she's some kind of religious nut-case. Provokes three guys to gang-rape her, then spills this yarn about the anti-God sailors and the desecrated cross. A new saint is born. Maybe they'll even name a street after her.'

Sullivan almost sighed with relief. But not yet. This could be a try-on by Summers, to open him up and get a peek at his own slant on the story. He said, 'You might have something there, Ed. It's at least as tenable as that other theory going the rounds.'

'What other theory?'

'That it was a put-up job, by the CIA.'

'Ah, c'mon Bob! Ten years ago I might have bought that, but the boys have got themselves a little refinement since then. A stroke like that only has to backfire for Washington to be knee-deep in rolling heads.'

'Maybe. But a desperate situation can spawn desperate resorts. The Soviet Fleet has got to be sent packing. So has Paul Spitari. And soon, Ed—before the Maltese get used to having them around.'

'Well I'll tell you what. You work on the CIA angle and I'll stick to the religious hysteria. Neither of us is going to make the Reader's Digest but at least we won't be treading on each other's heels.' He had twisted around in his chair and was signalling to a waiter. 'Let's do a bit of armchair public-opinion polling, while we're about it.'

The waiter stood in front of them. He was a young man with a studious air to him. A university student, conceivably, working his way through college.

Summers said, 'This affair of the Russian sailors, my friend. What do you think the government should do about it?'

'Do?' The waiter's neck had gone stiff; his eyes blazed behind the thick lenses. 'There's only one thing to do, isn't there? We should ask the American Sixth Fleet to blast those bloody Reds right out of the Mediterranean!'

'You've no doubt whatsoever the girl really was raped by Russian sailors?' Sullivan asked mildly.

'Doubt?' the waiter shrilled. 'You think a decent girl would tell lies about something like that?'

'You're right, man. Just what I was telling my friend here. Would you like to bring us another bottle of champagne?'

3

I

The two English-language newspapers came in with his breakfast tray. From the bathroom, Sullivan called to the waiter to
leave the tray on the desk and, a minute later, padded out
damp and cool from the shower and sank the tall glass of
orange juice in one long grateful gulp. The champagne-thirst
was still with him. He started to pour the coffee, meantime
unfolding the first newspaper, *The Times of Malta*, and
quickly scanning the Archbishop's statement, set out in bold
double-column longprimer under the banner-heading

OUR CHRISTIAN HERITAGE AT STAKE

The language had dignity, obvious sincerity, and compassion,
even for the 'wretched sinners—their spirits so perverted by
atheistic materialism as to put in question their right to be
described as human beings'. Nevertheless they did have im-

mortal souls and were capable—as all God's children were—of redemption. The people of Malta, in their rightful anger at this foul deed done to one of their daughters, were entitled to demand temporal justice and the punishment of the wrongdoers. At the same time, as good Catholics they should spare a prayer for those who had been denied the birthright of baptism and the civilising grace of the Christian ethic.

The Archbishop saved his thunder for the last few paragraphs. These were directed at the leaders of the People's Party who, by an act of wanton political irresponsibility had antagonised Malta's true friends of the free and democratic Western community and exposed innocent young girls to dangers the like of which the inhabitants of this ancient fortress island had not had to face since its occupation by Napoleon's troops one-hundred-and-seventy years ago. The Archbishop's statement concluded with a reminder to the Prime Minister that he was the servant, not the master of the people. And the will of the people, as so clearly expressed in spontaneous demonstrations throughout the island, was that Malta should have done with the Soviet Fleet and any further truck with Nato's chief antagonist in the Mediterranean.

Sullivan put the *Times* to one side and unfolded the *Malta Mail*. The lead story was headed; LINA MAZZI: SOME DISTURBING DISCLOSURES. He read on.

The alleged multiple rape of eighteen-year-old Lina Mazzi has so shocked and angered the Maltese nation that, pending unforeseen disclosures in the full report of the investigation authorities, it might seem that the Prime Minister has little choice between denouncing the agreement with the Soviet Union relating to its use of Malta's harbours and resigning his office to make way for someone who will.

However, if Prime Minister Paul Spitari seems to be dragging his feet so far as positive retaliatory measures are concerned, it must be pointed out in his defence that the evidence of the alleged outrage rests for the moment solely on statements made by this young girl coupled with the medical report of the examining doctors at St

Luke's hospital. There were, unfortunately, no independent witnesses. Identification of the alleged rapists has not yet been possible. And a terse statement issued last night by the Commander of the Soviet warships categorically denies that any personnel of Soviet naval vessels were anywhere near the scene of the crime the night before last.

With the Prime Minister, this newspaper awaits—albeit impatiently—the official decision that a *prima facie* case exists for a charge of multiple-rape against certain Soviet sailors as yet unknown before adding our voice to those already calling for immediate and decisive diplomatic action. In the meantime, however, and with the sole motive of bringing all possible light to bear on this grave and explosive situation, the *Malta Mail* has been examining certain information bearing on the general character and credibility of Miss Lina Mazzi.

It would appear that, contrary to earlier reports leaked from Police Headquarters, the young girl was not *virgo intacta* at the time of the alleged raping but in fact had had a childbirth aborted by a private medical practitioner only four months previously. Further evidence made available to this newspaper by reliable sources last night casts positive doubt on the official police description of Miss Mazzi as a 'respectable' young woman.

We have deemed it proper not to publish details of this evidence while the circumstances of the alleged crime are still under investigation, but these details were handed over last night to the police officer in charge of the case. We emphasize that nothing in this new evidence about the character of Miss Mazzi could remotely justify, or mitigate the seriousness of, the crime alleged to have been committed against her. The purpose of this statement is to lend support to those—including, we believe, the Prime Minister—who are counselling public restraint until all the relevant facts become available.

40

Sullivan poured himself another cup of coffee and took it over to the window. Carona was taking a hell of a chance. Quite apart from the libel aspect, he and his newspaper were swimming against a tide of popular feeling that would swamp them if these insinuations against Lina Mazzi couldn't be proved to the hilt. He looked at his watch. It was far too early yet to wake up an editor who most probably hadn't got to bed before two o'clock that morning. He would be seeing him, anyway, at the Prime Minister's press conference in the Auberge d'Aragon in a couple of hours. Meantime, there was the story of his adventure aboard *The Gurkha* to type out and airmail to the agency's Features department...

He had punched out about two thousand words and was starting on a fresh pot of coffee when the telephone rang from the bedside. It was the operator, asking if he would take a call from Miss Safad.

'Put her on, please.'

He had put on a shirt and pants before settling down to work. Her voice, with its slight accent and warm feminine timbre, made him feel naked again.

'I just wanted to ask you if we are going anywhere—well, grand tonight. It is a question of what I should wear.'

'I don't know, Daria... Whatever you think would be *comme-il-faut* for a Wimpey Bar, I guess.'

'Listen, Mr Sullivan: I may belong to a persecuted minority, but if you think—'

'All right, all right! So you want to live it up, rub shoulders with the élite. And I had you down as one of those simple earthy birds from the kibbutz... How about the Tigullio for dinner and shaking it around the floor at Sacha's afterwards?'

'Now you are putting your money where your mouth is.'

'Daria, where does a nice girl like you pick up such vulgar expressions?'

'We meet a lot of Americans in Tel Aviv. Oh, I'm sorry—I keep forgetting.' There was a moment's pause. Then: 'I suppose you're very much involved in the Russian rape affair?'

'I'm covering it for my agency, yes. I imagine your own people are not exactly disinterested observers of the unfolding drama.'

There was a soft chuckle at the other end of the line. 'I'm sorry for the poor girl. But she'll be given a very sympathetic reception in Tel Aviv, if she ever decides to take a holiday there.'

'Have you seen this morning's *Malta Mail?*'

'Yes. I have it on my desk right here. It's absolutely disgraceful!'

'You think so?'

'I certainly do. Smearing the girl's character like that, just to make things easier for Paul Spitari!' There was another brief silence. He could imagine her face, the slight flush to her smooth cheeks; the big blazing eyes.

'I suppose you'll be going to his press conference this morning?'

'You bet. Matter of fact, I'd better start—'

'It's all right, I'm hanging up now. Till tonight, then.'

'Till tonight, Daria. Oh, and listen—'

'Yes, Bob?'

'It's groovy, talking to you over breakfast like this.'

'Correction. I've had mine, and I *never* talk until after breakfast.'

'I'll try to remember that.'

John Carona had kept a seat for him near one of the open windows of the conference-room at the Auberge d' Aragon. He was grateful for it, particularly when the TV lights went on.

The Prime Minister had just made his appearance and as the roomful of newsmen rose to their feet Sullivan took another look around and spotted Ed Summers, a late arrival, standing against the wall just inside the doorway. *Crafty sod. That must have been his stooge encamped in the incongruous red London-style telephone booth outside in Independence Square. An open line from there to the Hilton, where another stooge would be keeping a line open to New York.*

When the newsmen had settled back in their chairs, the Prime Minister began to read aloud from a prepared statement. His voice and manner were calmly authoritative.

'The events of the past thirty-six hours, gentlemen, have imposed a heavy strain on all of us and I would like to thank

42

those of you who have shown patience and a sense of responsibility in their professional attitude to this crisis in which we are all now involved.

'I ought to inform you, straightaway and before inviting your questions, that preliminary police inquiries into the allegations made by Miss Lina Mazzi are not yet complete—' He paused, turning his head to gaze solemnly out of the window as a hollow groan of exasperation went up from the body of the room. Sullivan, glancing across at Summers, watched the American's brow and lips contract in irritation.

'I understand your impatience, gentlemen,' Spitari resumed. 'I share it. But here in Malta, as in most civilised countries of the world, our affairs are conducted by the rule of law and in conformity with elementary principles of justice. We do not condemn until we have clear grounds for condemnation. We do not judge until we know precisely what it is we are judging. On the threshold—as we are today—of grave decisions, with even graver international repercussions, we must pause to arm ourselves with the truth, and the *whole* truth, before taking that final and perhaps irrevocable step forward.

'I am advised by the Commissioner of Police that the report of his investigating officers will be on my desk by not later than five o'clock this evening. I have consequently made arrangements to appear on Malta television this evening to inform my fellow-countrymen and women of the steps their government proposes to take in the light of this report.'

And with a slight bow to the room, the Prime Minister sat down.

A dozen newsmen were on their feet at once. Spitari waved them down and nodded to a bushy-haired man who remained standing in the front row. 'Let *The Times of Malta* get in first, gentlemen. One appreciates how concerned they must be to alleviate their readers' anxiety.' Over a rustle of laughter the voice of the man from *The Times of Malta* rang out, clear and aggressive.

'In view of the Prime Minister's stirring tribute to the rule of law and the elementary principles of justice, will he please give us his reaction to the vicious and cowardly assault on the

43

character of Lina Mazzi in this morning's issue of the *Malta Mail*?'

From Carona, seated beside Sullivan, came a quiet 'Ouch!'

Paul Spitari was pursing his lips, frowning. 'If,' he said after a short silence, 'the report you refer to is unfounded, then the subject of it has recourse to the law and the provisions of justice. If there should be any substance to it, then I welcome it as a potentially vital contribution to our evaluation of the events of last Monday night.'

'But this is monstrous—!' The *Times* man shot to his feet again. 'Not a scrap of real evidence was—'

'All right!' Spitari cut in, waving the reporter down. 'I've given you my answer . . . You, sir!' He pointed to Ed Summers who, one arm raised, had moved a step away from the wall.

'Ed Summers. United Press International. We appreciate, Mr Prime Minister, that the Malta police have no power to enforce identification-parades aboard the Soviet ships. Would you not agree, however, that it would be a mark of good faith and a powerful contribution to the lessening of tension if the Soviet authorities would give their consent to this?'

'In principle,' Spitari began, choosing his words carefully, 'I would agree with what you say. I have in fact made strong representations to the Soviet ambassador to that effect. However—.' He fell silent for a moment. Then: 'I want to deal with this point, but in fairness to Miss Mazzi I think this had better be off-the-record.' His eyes ranged the room. 'Is that agreed, gentlemen?' There was a murmur of reluctant assent. 'If anyone objects to it being off-the record will he please raise a hand?'

The Times of Malta man swung his head around to study the rest of the room. No one had raised a hand. He gave a shrug and settled back in his chair.

'The Soviet authorities,' Spitari continued, 'are in a difficult position over this. As you already know, they categorically deny that any of their personnel were anywhere near the scene of the alleged rape. Several hundreds of their ratings were not even on shore that night, and of course if Miss Mazzi, through—what shall I say?—a defective memory?—should positively identify any of *these* men as her assailants then the police would have no case to present to court. However, let us suppose she identifies—to her own satisfaction, anyway—one or more of the men known to have been ashore that night. And let us suppose that person's alibi is not acceptable to our police. The precedent, gentlemen, was laid down not so long ago by the United States Navy in the instance of one of their naval ratings, accused of the murder of a Maltese prostitute. The person or persons identified would have to be handed over to our police to stand trial on the territory where the crime was committed. They would have to be defended by Maltese lawyers. The Soviet authorities, to put it mildly, are not convinced there would be a fair trial.'

'So what's the alternative, sir?' A North American voice called out from behind Sullivan. 'Are they going to be allowed to just up-anchor and go?'

Spitari was shaking his head. 'They realise that if they do that, before our inquiries are complete, they can never return to our harbours. My own belief is that the Soviet Government has already given instructions to their naval commander here to cooperate fully with the police should their findings produce a *prima facie* case against sailors under his command.'

'*For* the record, Signor Spitari—' it was a reporter from *Oggi* who had caught the Prime Minister's eye '—do you now, speaking frankly, regret your decision to invite the Soviet fleet here, against the interests of the Nato states?'

Spitari's strained nerves were beginning to show. There was a film of sweat across his brow and he was having trouble keeping his hands at rest. 'No, I do not regret that desision,' he growled. 'What I *would* regret would be having to reverse it, in highly emotional circumstances, for reasons which have no direct bearing on the broader issues of—of national self-interest that promoted the decision in the first place.'

The Times of Malta man was on his feet again. 'Are you telling us, sir, that a savage and unprovoked attack on a young Maltese girl by a gang of lustful and blasphemous communist sailors...'

'I'll buy you lunch at the Union Club,' Carona said, manoeuvring his car out of the parking area of Palace Square.

'The food's appalling but you haven't lived till you've seen the types we get there these days.'

'How do you think Spitari made out?'

'A passable back-to-the-wall performance. He'll do better on TV tonight, I hope, with the police report in his pocket.'

'Confirming your "disturbing disclosures" about Lina Mazzi?'

'They can hardly ignore the stuff I've handed them. Just watch the heat go out of this case when the mums and dads and aunties hear what a right little raver we've got in Lina Mazzi. I understand the Archbishop has already decided to tone down his directive to the parish priests since we spilled the beans this morning.'

'What are the actual facts, John?'

Carona took a light from Sullivan and drew deeply on his cheroot. The car immediately ahead of them turned off left into Castile Place, its right-hand indicator flashing busily away.

'Did you hear about the one and only Maltese motorist who ever got to heaven?'

'I'll buy it,' Sullivan sighed.

'He was invited to sit at God's right hand but took so long trying to work it all out he lost his place to an upstart American cardinal.'

'A gas. Can we get back to Miss Mazzi—'

'What do you want to know?'

'Who tipped you off? Is she a whore, an enthusiastic amateur, or what?'

'Not exactly a whore. Let's say she's been discreetly generous with her favours to any like-spirited recipients thereof. Her job as a room-maid at the Europa opened it all up for her. Texan oil-men from Tripoli, British and German businessmen, the better-heeled type of tourist. It was an oil man who got her pregnant. She went on the pill after that, so there won't be any little Russian bastard sucking at her tits in nine months' time—assuming it *was* Russians who put in the old pork sword.'

'Didn't she have any Maltese gentlemen friends?'

'Apparently not. It's a small island and the word gets

around very quickly. She didn't want her family to know what she was up to. We'd probably all still be in the dark if it hadn't been for this phone call I got from London.'

There were two cars ahead of them as they descended towards Pieta. The one in the fast lane was doing about twelve miles-an-hour; the car in the slow lane was keeping abreast of the other. Carona leaned on his horn. The driver in the fast lane slowed perceptibly down; he of the slow lane shot ahead like a getaway car from a smash and grab raid.

'There's another yarn about Maltese drivers. It seems—. What's the mater, Bob?'

'The phone call from London, John. For cryin' out loud!'

'Ah, yes. Fellow I went to school with in Mill Hill. He flies to Malta quite often. Something to do with a paper factory here. We don't see much of each other but he drops in to the office once in a while for a chat. Anyway, he gave me most of the dope about Lina Mazzi. He's a dead truthful bloke and according to him, she can't get enough of it. On top of which she's a pathological liar. Told him she'd had Prince Charles *and* Princess Anne when they paid that visit to the island . . . A royal flush, no less.'

Sullivan chuckled, then fell silent as Carona weaved in and out of the traffic on Savoy Hill. It was all very interesting but it wasn't helping him to establish the Burgo-Mazzi connection. He toyed for a moment with the thought of letting John in on what he knew. He would probably get what he wanted a lot faster with his friend's help; but . . . It was his story. A world beat. He'd wrap it up somehow.

They parked in the spacious Union Club forecourt and Carona shepherded him across the imposing entrance-hall and into the bar. 'They call this place "God's waiting-room",' Carona muttered on the way. 'You'll see why in a minute.'

The bar ran down one complete side of a vast high-ceilinged room and, spread three- or four-deep throughout its length, was the largest assembly of British expatriates Sullivan had ever seen under one roof in Malta. And the oldest. At a quick guess he would have put the average age at sixty, with a starting minimum of forty-five. These, of course, were the New Residents, or Sixpenny Settlers—refugees from Britain's stiff unearned-income taxation who had retired to Malta to live on their capital or dividend income and enjoy the island's tax levy of a mere sixpence in the pound.

While Carona fought for the drinks, Sullivan scanned the room for the sight of a young face, or at least one that might have looked out of place at a Tory veteran's rally. He scanned in vain. The eyes that turned to him, studying *him* with a kind of caged-in curiosity, were eyes that had never peered beyond the *Daily Telegraph* company reports, the novels of Galsworthy, the bar-chits of their lost Empire and *Hymns Ancient and Modern*.

'You're right,' he grunted as Carona thrust a gin-and-tonic in his hand. 'This lot gives you the creeps. It's like being stuck on a cruise-liner chartered by a geriatric clinic. What do these people do with themselves all day, apart from boozing at the Union Club?'

'Booze at one another's villas. "My turn Saturday, your turn Tuesday", sort of thing. It's a kind of tipsy gavotte —occasionally enlivened by a spasm of réchauffé randiness.'

'Why the hell are *you* a member, John?'

'Because I like to come here and sneer, of course . . . Drink up and we'll grab a table before the herd lifts its snout out of the watering-hole.'

After lunch, Carona drove him to the housing site where the gang-rape of Lina Mazzi had taken place. The road—if one could call it that—was unsurfaced and pitted with holes and it ended about fifty yards past the scene of the crime at a low stone wall with one narrow gap in it.

'There's just a track through there, dropping down to the Europa Hotel,' Carona explained, reversing his car up the ramp of a half-finished villa. 'That's the way Miss Mazzi came the night she copped it.'

'Hold it a second, John.' Sullivan started to open his door. 'I'll get out here and walk down to the hotel.' It was a sudden decision and there was no particular motive to it; it just seemed the right thing to do, being so near to Lina's workplace.

'I can drive around down and wait for you, Bob, if you're not going to be too long.'

48

'Thanks, but—you get on to the office. I'll take a cab back.'

The track wound down between stunted palms and oleander bushes and levelled out to skirt the tall wire fence of a tennis-court. Beyond this terrace a flight of steps led down to the pool area, where half-a-dozen assorted human shapes were laid out on mattresses, well-oiled and far gone in post-prandial torpor. Sullivan knew now what he had to do. Through a side-entrance of the main building he passed along a short corridor connecting with the reception hall. The man behind the desk was yawning into the mouthpiece of a telephone between grunts of *'Iva ... iva ... tajjeb ...'* He hung up and turned a resigned face to Sulivan.

'Sir?'

'I want to have a word with your staff-manager. Where do I find him?'

'Manager*ess*, sir. You can try her office. Third door on the right down there.' He pointed limply to a passageway across on the opposite side of the reception hall.

'Her name, please?'

'Mrs Faraclas, sir.'

'Sounds Greek.'

The man stifled a yawn. 'You're quite right, sir.'

There was no name on the door—just the words *Staff Control* in black lettering on a white plaque. Sullivan turned the handle and stepped in. The room was empty except for its steel desk, visitor's chair, filing-cabinet and a key-board attached to the wall behind the desk. While he hesitated, undecided whether to wait or go back to the reception desk, there came through a connecting-door to the right of the room a sound painfully evocative of Sullivan's schooldays, followed by a plaintive female cry of distress.

'Please, Madame! No more!'

Then a second voice—husky, heavily-accented:

'You rather I cut your wages this week?'

'No, Madame!'

'Then keep still!'

As Sullivan, eyebrows up, backed out of the room, the flesh-flinching sound was repeated, three more times. He closed the door behind him and sauntered slowly on along the passageway. He turned when he heard the door opening again and had to back quickly against the wall to avoid collision with a young girl in a short-skirted pink cotton smock who came running past him, head down and stifling a sob.

This time, he knocked and waited for a husky 'Come in!' before pushing open the door.

'Mrs Faraclas?'

The woman standing framed in the open connecting-door nodded and flicked a loose tassel of ash-blonde hair obscuring one of her amber-coloured eyes. She was in her early thirties, deep-breasted and beginning to spread at the hips; but if the waist was still her own, and not some corsetted imposter, Mrs Faraclas had the makings of a splendid hour-glass for the measuring of any man's siesta. Her sallow features, darkly flushed at this moment, were already on the slippery slope from beauty to dissoluteness. She was of the mould of one of those Greek or French 'Oedipal' actresses so revered by the more fastidious genre of film-critic.

'My name's Bob Sullivan. Can you spare me a few minutes?'

'By all means.' She eased a cigarette from the pack in her hand and raised it to her lips. 'Do you have a light, Mr Sullivan?'

He found his lighter and she advanced a couple of steps to meet him. The fingers supporting the cigarette were shaking slightly and at this close quarter Sullivan could see the darker nap at the roots of her hair and smell the musk blend of armpit sweat and deodorant.

'Are you a guest of the hotel?' She had moved to behind her desk and was gesturing toward the visitor's chair.

'No, I'm at the Phoenicia.' He handed her his card and sat down. 'I'm covering the Lina Mazzi story for my agency.'

'I see . . .' She lowered herself into her chair and propped his card with exaggerated care against a pen-holder. All her movements—like her voice—were slow, as if weighted by caution. 'And you want to—what is the word?—*pump* me about the poor child?'

'I'd like to ask you a few questions.'

She gave no reply. She was leaning back now, watching him

50

with eyes slotted by the smoke curling from her cigarette. The smile was defensive. He took it as an encouragement to go ahead.

'Had you any idea, Mrs Faraclas, of the kind of life Lina led outside working hours?'

She hesitated a moment before shaking her head. 'No ... You see, Mr Sullivan, I took this job on only three weeks ago.'

'I didn't realise that. May I ask where you were working before?'

'In Athens. For another hotel under the same management. They wanted someone to teach the girls here some efficiency, so—' she shrugged and leaned forward to tap the ash from her cigarette '—I took the job on for a—change of scene?'

'Tell me—any outside messages for the girls—I mean during working hours—would they receive them through you, Mrs Faraclas, or the hotel switchboard?'

'The switchboard would give me the messages. I am very strict about that.'

'Then you would know if there were any messages for Lina Mazzi last Monday, before she finished work?'

'Naturally ... As a matter of fact, I think there *was* one. A man. I can't remember his name.'

'Does the name Burgo ring any kind of bell?'

'Burgo? No-o, I don't think so.'

'Wouldn't you have written the name down?'

'Certainly. There was a phone number, too, for her to call back. I remember scribbling it on that pad there and giving it to the head girl to give to Lina.'

'This is very important to me, Mrs Faraclas. Could we have the head girl in for a minute, to see if she remembers the name?'

'I will ask her tomorrow. She is in Gozo today, visiting her sister in some convent there.' Mrs Faraclas stubbed out her cigarette and stood up. 'You will forgive me, Mr Sullivan? I have a great deal of work to do.'

'You've been very kind.' He put out his hand and she took it briefly in a strong, surprisingly cool grasp. 'May I call you in the morning?'

'Not before nine o'clock, please. Goodbye, Mr Sullivan.'

51

He had intended to take just one hour's siesta before checking with John Carona on latest developments. He came awake once, peered at his watch and rolled over to a cooler patch of the bed. When he woke up again it was six-thirty.

Three minutes under the cold shower took the lead out of his limbs and now, as he shaved, he let his thoughts dwell for a while on his date with Daria that evening ... What did he want from her, apart from the gift of her flesh? A revelation? A sudden suspension of lust, in which to hear himself telling her, with honesty, he had fallen in love with her? It was not so remote a possibility; there was a great deal about Daria that stirred the romantic in him, that might so easily tap the source of that almost-forgotten, helpless euphoria by which a man measures the collapse of all emotional autonomy. That she was dark-haired and lovely and able to communicate as potently through her eyes as her tongue—these were grave enough threats to his defences. That she was intelligent, with a gently ironic turn of humour, could only increase his vulnerability. Her background—surely, with a name like Safad, a native citizen of her brave new state—supplied for Sullivan the indispensable allure—part charisma, part challenge—without which her body, however young and nubile, could engage little more than his lust and the ego that was partner to it. He thought of Mia ... of the wounds, still raw, of that shattering betrayal. There could be for him only one physic with the power to heal, to erase. Perhaps ... yes, perhaps ...

The telephone rang out in the bedroom. It was a call from London. Bill Topper.

'How's it coming, mate?'

'Haven't cracked it yet, Bill. Got a new lead, though, and I'm hoping it'll open up something tomorrow. You got Carona's telex on Lina's love-life, and the PM's comments?'

'Yep. Look, the story's very big here, Bob. And in the States, of course. Anything new you can feed us—'

'You'll just have to be patient, Bill. This is a hot one and I don't want to come off half-cock. When's that help I asked for getting here?'

'On tonight's BEA flight. Fred Fairchild. You want to talk to him?'

'Not particularly. Tell him to get his briefings from John Carona and to keep right out of my hair. He's on his own till I contact him, dig?'

'Dig ... Want any money?'

'I'm all right for now. Don't fret if you don't hear from me for a day or two. It won't mean I've stopped loving you.'

'I shall be borne up by that thought. Take good care, sweetheart.'

After padding back to the bathroom to wash the shaving-cream from his face, Sullivan put in a call to Carona. He told him about Fairchild, explaining that he himself might be called off the Mazzi story to cover the new outbreak of riots in Rome, and then asked Carona what time Prime Minister Spitari would be making his TV appearance that evening.

'Seven-forty-five. You want to catch it here in my office?'

'Thanks, but—' He remembered Daria's mentioning she had TV. He could phone copy through to Carona from her place, if the statement called for any interpretative stuff. With a cold drink in his hand. In her bedroom, maybe, before giving a helping hand with the zip?

'That's under control, John. One thing, though—can you give me the name of the US Embassy's CIA contact? At the top.'

'Just a second ... Well, it's supposedly a commercial attaché called Walter Masters, but you know how it is. You can certainly start with him, anyway.'

'Thanks, pal. Look after Fairchild. His old man's one of our vice-presidents.'

'I'll cosset him. Don't do in Rome anything the Romans wouldn't do.'

It was six-fifty-five. He'd have to get it together fast to finish dressing, find a cab and be at Daria's villa before seven-forty-five. No time now to go hunting for that promised peace-offering. Well, maybe a bottle of champagne off the *sommelier* down in the restaurant ...

The wine-waiter had been obliging and the bottle was

delivered to him, ice-cold, as he cashed some traveller's cheques at the front desk. But it was a warm night, with the temperature up in the eighties, and the chill had gone from the bottle long before his taxi made the descent to Baluta Bay. They drove on around St Julian's Bay, then up to skirt Paceville and swing left onto the main coast road to the island's north-western beaches; and it was only as the taxi slowed down and Sullivan caught sight of the St Andrews Barracks complex below the road to his right that it came to him, with an obscure disquiet, that this was just about the spot where the ravished Lina Mazzi had been picked up by the English motorist from Madliena.

They were turning into a steeply-rising narrow dirt road honeycombed with craters, and the driver muttered an oath as he spotted another car picking its way towards them. As the two vehicles slowed to a crawl before passing each other, Sullivan had barely time to identify the man in the passenger-seat, talking earnestly to the man at the wheel, before crouching quickly forward, pretending to fasten a shoelace. It was Alfonso Burgo...

He straightened up as his taxi rattled on over the bumpy crown of the road and stared ahead, vaguely registering the scatter of villas over the rising ground to either side of him. Burgo... the scene of the crime, near enough halfway between the Europa and this neck of the woods... Daria Safad coming out of that side-door from Police Headquarters yesterday, with Detective-Inspector Avanzo and Lina Mazzi inside... Her words, four days ago in the Blue Lounge of the Phoenicia, rushed back at him: 'That's not how we see it in my country. Spitari has handed our worst enemy—after the United Arab Republic—a staging-post in the Middle Sea.'

There was a fork coming up just ahead, and one of the roads would lead to the Villa Margarita. There was no way of knowing whether Burgo had been coming from there or from someone totally unconnected with Daria, and without knowing this, all the rest could be either coincidental or immaterial. But the possibility was clearly there. Beautiful Israeli agent. Wine-exporter promotion as clever 'cover'. Working with the CIA—as a trusted broker, maybe, between them and their Maltese hirelings. It was all just too damned possible, and it was a worm already burrowing into his ego, for if it were true it meant her interest in him (*'I suppose you're very much involved in the Russian rape affair'*) started and stopped at his international press credentials and the doors and mouths these were able to open.

The taxi came to a halt at a pair of wrought-iron gates set in a low stone wall. There was a short driveway leading to the villa's front door and then on to a bamboo-roofed car-port built between two gnarled old carob trees. Daria's car was backed into the port.

'You want me to drive in, sir?'

'This'll do fine.' He jumped out and handed the driver a pound-note. 'No need to wait, thank you.'

He was on the point of pressing the visitors' bell a second time when the door opened halfway and Daria's head came around it, black hair pinned up, blue-grey eyes rounded in good humoured astonishment.

'M*adonna*!'—it was a perfect take-off of the standard Maltese ejaculation—'You're so early!'

'Sorry, Sergeant. The Prime Minister's on TV in a few minutes and I thought I'd catch it here.'

'Why didn't you phone? I would have got ready earlier.'

'You never gave me your number ... Well, are you going to let me in?'

'Oh, dear! Just a second.' The hand holding the door disappeared and there was a flash of naked shoulder as she manipulated something out of sight. 'I only just got out of the bath ... There!' The door opened up and she waved him in and closed it quickly behind him. She had a pink bath-towel wrapped inadequately about her torso, and as she talked to him she was backing towards the staircase at the far end of the long rectangular hall.

'Make yourself at home in there.' She nodded towards the arched opening in the wall immediately to his right. 'The TV is already switched on. I wanted to be ready myself in time to hear that horror, Spitari.'

'What held you up—visitors?' He knew when his "easy" smile was on straight. It was on straight now—but only just.

She shook her head. She had stopped at the foot of the staircase, still facing him, with one hand clutching the towel to her bosom and the other holding the hem down over her crotch. 'I was late getting back from Valletta.'

They stayed where they were, facing each other from either end of the hall.

'Well, go on in!' she laughed. 'I can't go up these stairs while you're watching me!'

'Strange—' he shook his head. 'Never had you figured as a spoilsport. Oh, well—.' He put the bottle of champagne on the marble-topped hall-table and passed in under the archway. The TV set faced him from the centre of the far wall, where in colder climes the fireplace might have been. There was a king-size sofa to the left of it, facing the two high windows to Sullivan's right. A couple of armchairs faced the sofa across a low circular table in black marble. Two large Casa Pupo rugs glowed greenly from the tiled floor and an enormous relief-painting in interlocked abstract patterns vibrated at him from the wall above the TV. There was another, smaller archway in the wall behind the sofa and through it, a gleam of silver candlesticks from a glass-topped dining-table.

A woman announcer was just rounding off something in Maltese. She paused, consulted her notes, then looked up again into the camera.

'In a few moments the Prime Minister, Mr Paul Spitari, will be making a special appearance. In view of the international interest in this matter and the presence in Malta of a great number of journalists from other countries, the Prime Minister will speak first in Maltese and then immediately afterwards in English.' The picture was cut and a still photograph of the Auberge d'Aragon took its place. As this, in turn, gave way to a stock film-shot of the Maltese flag streaming from its flagpole, there came the music-over of the Maltese national anthem—measured, solemnly architectural. *This is ominous,* Sullivan thought. *He's either about to declare war on Russia or else announce the arrest of Lina Mazzi for corrupting Soviet sailors* ... Then Spitari's head and shoulders filled the screen and his gruff voice prowled the room.

'*Hbjeb ... Il lela inkellimkton ...*'

56

Sullivan was standing in the middle of the room, staring up at the relief-painting, when Daria joined him. Spitari was speaking in Maltese.

'Do you want to buy it, Bob?' Her hair was loose about her shoulders. The dress was apple-green and closely tailored to her superb figure. His eyes made a slow inventory of her. 'I wouldn't mind,' he murmured, 'having it on approval for a few nights.'

'The *painting*—idiot!' she laughed. 'What do you think of it?'

'I like it immensely. Whose work?'

'A Maltese artist called Gabriel Caruana. He sculpts, too —fabulous abstract objects. I'm arranging an exhibition of his work in Israel.' She strode to the grog-trolley beside the archway into the dining-room. 'What can I offer you to drink?'

'Scotch-on-the-rocks, please.'

'I put that lovely bottle of champagne in the refrigerator. Thank you, Bob.' She took his drink over to him. 'We'll drink it together some time.'

'I'm holding you to it.'

Their eyes unlocked as Spitari's speech in Maltese ended. Sullivan put his glass down and plucked a thin note book from his hip pocket. Daria turned away, smiling, and crossed over to one of the armchairs.

The PM's TV manner was just right—grave without being pompous. He spoke slowly, in a tone that carried conviction, leading off with a recapitulation of the circumstances in which his government had decided to open Malta's harbours and shore facilities, in time of peace, to the Soviet Mediterranean Fleet. He listed the trade and other economic benefits that had already begun to flow from this decision. He recalled the nervousness with which the Maltese had awaited the fleet's maiden visit and their relief at the way in which the Russian sailors had comported themselves ashore—quoting with nicely-calculated effect from the laudatory editorial that had appeared in *The Times of Malta*. Dismissing the 'battle of Strait Street' as an unfortunate and perhaps inevitable consequence of the US President's 'hasty, and in the opinion of

57

many, unnecessarily provocative stage-managing of a coincidental American presence', the Prime Minister then turned to the case of Miss Lina Mazzi.

He touched briefly on her account of what had happened to her on Monday night, punctiliously attaching the adjective 'alleged' to every relevant verb. He read out from his notes, without nuance, the brief statement by the Soviet naval commander refuting the possibility of any Soviet involvement, and he then referred, with a perceptible hardening of tone, to the slurs by the *Malta Mail* upon the girl's character and credibility. 'These insinuations,' he growled, 'bring no honour to the newspaper that disseminated them.' With consummate cunning, the veteran politician went on to repeat the insinuations in the tone of a parent naively outraged by malicious whisperings against the honour of his own daughter. It was apparently true, 'but utterly irrelevant' that Miss Mazzi had had an abortion performed on her four months ago. Surely, in this day and age, there was nothing so wicked, or unpardonable, about that. As to the innuendos about promiscuity, and worse, the investigating police officer had 'up till now found no concrete evidence to support these defamatory, so-called "revelations" . . .'

As Spitari drew breath, Sullivan snatched a quick glance at Daria. She was leaning forward in her chair, eyes fixed on the screen, her lovely face stiff with distaste.

The Prime Minister had kept the real news for the end. The commander of the Soviet vessels at anchor in Malta had that afternoon agreed to invite the police to supervise identification parades in two days' time in each of the Soviet ships and to allow Miss Mazzi on board for that purpose. The short delay in staging the parades was at the request of the Maltese police, to enable them to make a thorough preliminary check of each ship's complement to ensure a hundred percent muster of the crews. Pending the outcome of these confrontations, the Prime Minister concluded, he would be acting in the best interests of the people of Malta by resisting pressure from all quarters, 'national and international', to intervene on the political or diplomatic level.

The picture faded on the PM collecting together his notes.

'And with that thought,' Sullivan observed, putting away his notebook, 'he wishes all his viewers a happy and non-controversial Christmas.'

'He is buying time,' Daria snapped, springing up. 'The man's nothing but a stooge of the Soviet Union.'

'Isn't that a bit on the harsh side, ma'am? Given an honest wish to keep Malta neutral—which I think is true of Spitari—isn't that just how most of us would play it?'

'Well, *he* may be neutral and so may *you*, Mr Sullivan'—her eyes blazed at him—'but I'm not, and in my opinion the man is showing himself to be a political simpleton!'

'May I quote you on that—as coming from "one Israel —um—agent close to government circles"?'

If she caught any inference in his choice of words, she was not rising to it. She pulled a face at him and scooped up his empty glass.

'Another drink?'

'Just a weak one, while I make a phone call—is that all right?'

'It's out in the hallway. Be my guest, as they say.'

He heard the TV being switched off as he dialled the *Malta News*. It would have been an action without particular significance were it not for the fact that she had cut the transmission in the middle of a commercial for Israeli wines . . . He spoke up loudly when John Carona came on the line and, after discussing the PM's statement with him, Sullivan dictated a few paragraphs as 'head and tail' for the telex cable to London. Then, in a voice carefully lowered but intended to be audible in the room behind him, he said, 'Any more dirt on Lina Mazzi, John?'

'You kidding? You heard the Prime Minister tearing those strips off me. I'm sitting here in sackcloth and ashes.'

'Is that so . . . You've got their names and everything?'

'What the hell are you talking about?'

'Very interesting. Thanks, John. I'll be seeing you.' And he hung up.

Daria handed him his drink with a smile, then crossed the room to close and fasten the windows.

59

'Was the great editor pleased with his paymaster's effort?' she called back over her shoulder.

'He's wincing a bit from the public ticking-off he got. But quite unpenitent.'

She turned back to face him. She could have said, 'What's that creep cooking up now against that poor girl?' or something to that effect. She said, 'Is this dress all right for the Tigullio? I've never been there.' And, suddenly, he began to feel a lot better.

II

He had commented, as they turned onto the coast road by St Andrew's Barracks, about the closeness of her villa to the scene of the rape, and she had nodded and given a little shudder.

'Don't remind me of it. It might so easily have been me.'

Now, as they faced each other across a table at the Tigullio, he tried telling himself he was gazing into the eyes of a ruthless undercover agent. And he told himself, right back, that he wouldn't swallow that washed down with Tokay Essenz. For more than ten years now he had been chasing the Big Story thoughout the civilised and savage world and in that time he had rubbed shoulders one way or another with more secret agents than most newsmen had had hangovers. He had been fooled once or twice, but only for as long as it took those tell-tale antennae of his to start vibrating, which had usually been on a second or third encounter. This was his third meeting with Daria Safad. She was still a stranger to him, and there was certainly no rational basis to it, but as he watched her now, the movement of her lips as she spoke, the changes of expression in her eyes, the gestures of her slim hands, he needed nothing but his own intuition to tell him *this* girl was no phoney.

'. . . So finally, three years ago, they got so fed up with me they said, "All right, little Jew-girl, if you want to go that much, then go! You can take one suitcase with you and a second eyepatch to stick on Moshe Dayan".' Daria took a sip of wine, her eyes twinkling at Sullivan over the rim of the glass. 'You know what I told them? I said, "With *two* eyes covered

General Dayan could still make rings around your Egyptian camel-drivers!" '

'You're lucky they didn't tear up your exit-visa... Did you ever get to meet your hero?'

'With a whole company of other girls, yes. He visited our training camp, a few weeks after I started my military service. Marching past him, with those other girls from so many different countries—it was like a dream come true for me.'

'Didn't you want to stay on in the army after your service was over?'

'I would have been very happy to. But because of this viniculture training I'd had, back in the Georgian Republic, they decided I'd be more useful to them in the Department of Agriculture. So I didn't argue with them and—well—see where it has got me!' She rolled her eyes in mock despair. 'Drinking Soave with an Irish journalist in Malta, GC!'

He said, 'Is that really so bad?'

She looked down at her plate, at the neglected *saltimbocca alla Romana,* then up, straight into his eyes. She wasn't smiling. 'Does that need an answer, Bob?' she asked softly.

He moved his hand across the table and took hold of hers and held it tightly for a long moment...

He ordered *zabaglione* for them both and, after the table had been cleared, some *Bols Kirschwasser* to clear their palates. The Italian pop-group had taken a break and there were several couples on the floor dancing in close embrace to canned music in smooch tempo.

'I have two left feet,' he said, 'but this happens to be their kind of music.'

'It's mine, too.' She got up and as he followed her between the tables, observing the slow swing of her hair and the movement of her hips behind the thin fabric of her dress, he said to himself, *And you're mine, for tonight anyway; and it's one of the best things that's happened to me in years.*

As they circled the darkened floor she made no provocative use of breasts or thighs, leaving it to him to control the closeness of their embrace. But the feel of her smooth back against his hand, the scent of her hair and the passive invitation

61

of her untensed arms were received stimuli more potent than any teasing could be. And when, feeling his hardness against her, she raised her face to him with her eyes closed and her lips parted, he put his cheek against hers and breathed her name and heard his own, whispered through a brush of lips across his ear. He released her and they made their way without speaking back to the table. After settling the bill he said, smiling across at her, 'If you knew of a quiet and comfortable place where we could bank on finding a bottle of well-chilled champagne, I'd be willing to give Sacha's a miss tonight.'

'This is uncanny! You've just read my mind.'

Outside, as he was opening the car door for her, she murmured, 'There's just one thing, Bob—'

He turned to her.

'—this place we're going to for the champagne—there may be difficulty getting a taxi to take you back to your hotel tonight.'

Her head was lowered and in dark shadow. He reached out, found her chin and tilted it until her eyes were silver slits in the blurred oval of her face.

'Let's go,' he said.

They had each drunk two glasses from Sullivan's bottle and she was stretched out on the living-room sofa, looking up at him from the headrest of his lap. He had drawn her skirt up to bare her thighs to his caress and now, as she parted them a little wider, he brought his hand to rest at the warmth beneath the white nylon briefs and held it there for a while, palming the captive mound with gentle strength, as one might cup the pulsing breast of a bird. These, he told himself, were the best moments—not the violent engagement of flesh that was to come but these first tentative intimacies when a man's joy and duty lay in opening the play, in sounding the sensual responses of his partner.

She purred, and he drew the hand away and put it to her breasts, to each in turn, lightly stroking the thin cotton encasing them until he felt the crisp assertion of erupting tissue against his palm. She closed her eyes and murmured, 'Yes . . .'

as he unbuttoned the shirtwaister front from neck to hem and opened it up wide. Her nipples pushed darkly at the gauzy bra, and when he put his fingertips to their stiffness she drew in a quick breath and rolled her head against his stomach.

'You don't like?' he teased.

'I *love*!' And, arching her back: 'Undo the bra!'

She came once while he was kissing her breasts and then again, crying his name aloud, when he pulled her briefs down and put his hand to her. A minute later she sat up, shaking out her hair and wriggling free of the twisted dress.

'It has been very enjoyable, Mr Sullivan,' she said, leaning back and drawing his arms around her. 'Shall I try calling a taxi for you now?'

'What's wrong with driving me back yourself—ingrate.'

'Does that mean ungrateful?'

'Mm-hm.'

'So now you despise me?'

'With all my heart.'

'But not, I notice, with—*this*.'

'I'm not responsible for that. It has its own independent enthusiasms.'

'Like—for what I'm doing now?'

'It would certainly appear so.'

'But perhaps it is feeling a little claustrophobic, do you think?'

'How did you guess?'

She knelt then between his legs and unzipped him and he let his head fall back and closed his mind to let the pure physical ecstasy take over . . . All time dissolved. And when he felt he could bear no more of the torment except at the cost of his sanity, he made her stop and, throwing off his clothes, took her there on the green rug, riding her frenzied body to a shattering mutual climax.

After a while she got to her feet and gathered up their strewn clothes.

'Bring the wine upstairs,' she smiled back at him from the archway. 'I'll provide the woman and my bedside radio the song.'

He took his time, knowing she would be going first to the

63

bathroom to clean and refresh her body for him. There were pictures to look at in the hallway, small gilt-framed water-colours of Israeli landscapes, an intricate collage by Gabriel Caruana. He paused on the stairway landing to study the elaborate carving on the Maltese chest under the window. He wanted one just like this for his London pad and he must remember to ask Daria where he could get one. At the top landing he called to her and she answered him from the softly-lit interior beyond the half-open door to his right.

She was sitting at a dressing-table, brushing her hair. The covers of the wide low bed were turned down and the filmy curtains across the Venetian blinds were stirring to a slight breeze.

'There's a bathroom through that door over there,' she gestured with her brush. 'It's still in a mess, I'm afraid, from the panic you put me into, arriving so early this evening.'

He put the champagne and the one glass he was carrying on a table near the bed and walked over to stand behind her and gaze at her reflection in the mirror. He said, 'I have a bit of a problem, Daria. I think I'm becoming quite fond of you.'

She swung around on the stool and rose slowly to her feet to press the cool globes of her breasts against him. Their mouths came together. As they parted, she whispered, 'Let's not worry about such terrible problems for the moment, darling. Just take me to bed and teach me some more gratitude.'

Towards dawn he came out of deep oblivion to find the bedside light still on and Daria lying on her stomach, naked and pillowless, beside him. The air was cool now and he levered himself up on one elbow, blinking towards the foot of the bed for signs of a sheet; but it had obviously been kicked with the coverlet to the floor. As he hesitated, summoning the will to do something about it, Daria stirred and rolled over on her back without awakening. He examined her now from her tousled head to her wide-flung feet, at first with lazy tenderness and then, as his eyes drank deeper at the naked loveliness of the girl, with a sudden sharp renewal of lust. He took up his position, careful to keep his weight off her, and was halfway into her before her eyes fluttered open and her arms coiled about his neck, drawing him down . . .

When he woke up again there were slits of gold in the Venetian blinds and his wristwatch registered eight-fifteen. Daria was lying, curled and still, under the sheet they had draped their spent bodies with, and remembering her last drowsy words to him ('Public holiday tomorrow . . . sleep all morning . . .'), he rolled gently from the bed, found his clothes and took them into the bathroom, closing the door quietly behind him.

She hadn't stirred when he came out again, shoes in hand. He would leave her to sleep, make a note of her telephone number downstairs and call her later, after he had got the information he wanted out of Mrs Faraclas. But first—the Phoenicia and a long shower and change of clothes.

He stopped at the landing halfway down and squatted on the Maltese chest to pull on his shoes. Two things he must remember to ask her: about the chest and about the address of Gabriel Caruana's studio. They would go to the studio together after he had wrapped up this story and he would buy her a piece of sculpture and—he stood up, smiling, and turned around—perhaps the twin of this chest in which to store all those letters he intended mailing her from odd corners of the globe. He raised the lid of the chest and let it rest against the wall. The interior lining was of quilted red silk and, obeying no conscious impulse other than mild curiosity, he raised a corner of the rug folded on the top—then froze.

One of the white sailor's caps was stained dark around the sweat-band. The other two looked fairly clean. He lifted one up and read the gold Cyrillic letters stamped around the outside band of black ribbon, with his stomach bunching up and his mind a silent scream of protest. The three pairs of white pants were roughly bundled together, and when he shook them out it was the pair left in his grasp that had the bloodstains smudged about the crotch. He carefully replaced the uniforms and caps exactly as he had found them, then closed the lid and went down to wash his hands under the kitchen tap before letting himself out of the front door and striding off towards the coast road.

4

Of course he could refuse to believe it—until, at any rate, he heard it from her own lips. The sailor's uniforms could be explained away by telling himself they had been planted by Burgo, or his companion in that car, during their visit to the Villa Margarita last night. And why plant them on Daria? All right; how about this: Daria was, in fact, an Israeli under-cover agent. She had gone along with the conspiracy on the understanding the girl Lina would be molested—mildly assaulted, even—but certainly not brutally gang-raped as she had been. Now Daria, sickened by what had happened, was threatening to pull out. So the uniforms had been planted and Detective-Inspector Avanzo would get the 'tip-off' this morning and make his raid on the villa. And the price of Daria's freedom thereafter would be her silence—and strict obedience.

Good thinking, Sullivan ... Help yourself to the booby prize —a great big juicy Israeli lemon!

You could look at it another way. So she tricked the girl into coming to see her that night—or, more probably, to meet a well-heeled new admirer at the villa—knowing full well Lina Mazzi would be gang-raped to the point, conceivably, of permanent injury or death, but willing to condone the atrocity as a justifiable means to a noble end—the expulsion of the Soviet fleet from Malta. She was an Israeli citizen; a militant Zionist, most probably. The USSR was now her enemy. Was it such a monstrous crime she had committed, in the cause of patriotism and for so crucial an outcome? Could he not accept that there were, in fact, *two* Darias, each of them honest to herself in a differing context: the agent-Daria of 'my country, right or wrong' and the woman-Daria who had given herself to him so unstintingly, who had even deliberately passed up the opportunity to milk him of information vital to the conspiracy?

The answer to that theory greeted him half-an-hour after leaving the Villa Margarita, when he let himself into his room at the Phoenicia.

They had made a thorough job of it. His suitcase and grip had been diligently emptied of all contents and their interior linings ripped completely apart. The clothes from the wardrobe lay in a heap on the floor with their sleeves and pockets turned out and the ties slit down their seams. Every scrap of paper on his desk and in the drawers had been examined and tossed into a pile on the bed, which had first been stripped of all its covers and the mattress ripped open. The corners of the carpet were turned back, the pictures removed from the walls, his portable typewriter from its case. He looked into the bathroom. That, too, had been given a complete going-over. After all, he reflected bitterly, there had been no need for them to hurry. Hadn't they had Daria Safad's personal assurance he wouldn't be setting foot in his room again till this morning—if then? A DO NOT DISTURB sign on the door. A flask of coffee or whisky to sustain them at their labours. The bastards could have spent all night at it if they wished.

But what the hell were they looking for? His note-book, to establish how much he already knew about the conspiracy? That was safely in his hip-pocket—and, in any case, he wasn't that green an operator: there was nothing in the notebook about Peter Lund, Burgo, Avanzo, nor any *aide-mémoire* relating to anything not already publicly known about the Mazzi rape. The hot stuff had already gone on tape, and the tiny cassette, as always, been removed from the recorder and —. *The recorder . . . it would have given them at least a clue as to*—He spun around and started to hunt for it under the debris of papers, clothes and bedcovers. It had gone. The one thing in this room they had taken away with them. Unless . . .

He walked calmly over to the wardrobe and, raising his arm, began to feel into the left-hand corner above and behind the metal door-runners. This, as always, was where Bill Topper would find the taped guts of The Story—or as much of it as Sullivan had been able to put together—in the event of anything untoward happening to him. Here were the hard facts, the hypotheses, the interpretation.

The wood was still sticky from the strip of adhesive he had used. The cassette was gone.

He turned away and began, with robot deliberation, to sort out and tidy up the tangle of his belongings. His mind raced. These were no hamfisted local mercenaries who had gone over his room but professionals who knew all the tricks in the book. What was that John had once said about his own nation's police force? 'They wouldn't be able to find an oilrig in Grand Harbour.' It probably ruled out Burgo and Avanzo as his uninvited visitors but it sure as hell did not rule out the CIA. Well, there was something he might be able to do about that this morning. In the meantime he still had one lead not blown to the other side by the stolen tape—the message for Lina handled by the Greek butch-dyke with the penchant for chastising her young charges. 'Not before nine o'clock,' she had said. Well, it was now just ten minutes past.

It sounds, thought Sullivan, as Mrs Faraclas's voice came huskily affable over the line, as if she has caught a whole bunch of her maids out in some grave misdemeanour this morning.

'Ah yes, Mr Sullivan. You are in luck. My head girl remembers the name *and* the telephone number. You'll laugh when I tell you why. She plays the Lotto, you see, every week and she liked the sound of the man's telephone number!'

I'm laughing. Into the receiver, he said, 'That's great, Mrs Faraclas. Can I have it please?'

'Here it is. The name is Brecher and the number is 825471.'

'I'm very much obliged to you, Mrs Faraclas.'

'It's a pleasure, Mr Sullivan.'

He checked the telephone directory but there was no Brecher listed. It meant nothing; it was the latest book and it was already two years out of date. There might be a hang-up if it turned out to be an office number Brecher had given Lina to call back, for today and tomorrow were both public holidays, with only a few shops and foreign business-houses staying open. The way things were hotting up, he just hadn't two days' breathing-space before checking out Mr Brecher. He would have to call him now on the number the Greek butch had given him, hope to catch him in and play the whole thing by ear.

The calling-tone sounded for several seconds before a man's voice answered.

'Hello—yes?'

'Is that Mr Brecher speaking?'

'Brecher—yes.'

'Well, my name's Bob Sullivan, Mr Brecher, and I'd very much appreciate it if you could spare me a few minutes today. I work for an international news agency.'

'I don't understand. Why should you want to talk to me?' The voice—suddenly guarded—sounded Mittel-European, with North American overtones.

'I should prefer not to have to go into that over my hotel telephone, Mr Brecher. I—well, I believe it would be in your interest to meet me somewhere where we can talk in privacy.'

There was a long silence at the other end of the line. Then: 'Tell me one thing, please. Is it by any chance about a matter very much in the local news at the moment?'

'It is, Mr Brecher. But I haven't the slightest intention of bringing you any personal embarrassment. It's purely some incidental information I'm after.'

'I see . . . You promise, then, to keep my name completely out of this if I agree to meet you?'

'I promise.'

'I will assume you are a man of honour. Well, then—I shall be taking some photographs at the Hal-Safliena Hypogeum in Paola most of this morning. Would that be convenient?'

'Perfect. Shall we say some time between eleven and twelve?'

'Very well . . . Just one thing, Mr—er—'

'Sullivan.'

'One thing, Mr Sullivan. Who was it gave you my name and telephone number?'

'No one you need worry about. I'll explain when I see you. Thanks for your cooperation, sir.'

There were a dozen different aspects he ought to have been pondering as he showered and shaved, but his thoughts kept returning to the girl he had left sleeping in the Villa Margarita. The 'two-Darias' theory had now exploded right in his face. The girl who had threshed and groaned under him, whose scent was faintly upon him still, even as he towelled himself after the shower, was the girl who had deliberately decoyed him to allow her colleagues to take his room apart—just as surely as she had lured the unsuspecting Lina Mazzi to her villa on the night of the rape with an invitation to barter her flesh for some randy gentleman's largesse—most probably Mr Brecher's. He had yet to find out exactly how the conspirators had got wise to him, but this might easily have come about through Burgo's seeing him somewhere with Daria and recognising him as the tipsy 'engineer' inquiring about Peter Lund. Similarly, Daria's apparent rashness in holding onto the Soviet uniforms might have some simple explanation. What he still found difficult to accept was that the Israeli girl's ardent lovemaking, those passionate endearments—the tears of joy, even, after they had come together for the first time in her bedroom—that all this had been play-acting on her part. And if it hadn't been a charade, what kind of woman was it who could lavish those intimate caresses, frenzied climaxes and soft post-coital tendernesses on a man she knew to be possibly the one person bent on her betrayal. He was fighting a compulsion to wake her up with a telephone call, to congratulate her on the skill with which she had done her job of work last night, to let her believe he had known all the way along about her role in the conspiracy and that it was *he* who had been using *her* as a pawn. But that little luxury would have to stay on ice. As yet, she had no reason for believing he even suspected her of being involved in the Mazzi plot; his room, after all, could have been raided while he was out having dinner with any Tom, Dick or Mary last night. Well, let her go on believing that for the moment.

He put on the least crumpled of his clean shirts and a pair of lightweight chinos. Then he looked up the number of the US Embassy and put in a call.

'United States Embassy—good morning, sir!'

'I'd like to speak to Mr Walter Masters, please.'

'I'm sorry, but Mr Masters will not be coming in today.'

'Where can I get him? This is Bob Sullivan of Intercontinental News Bureaux. It's urgent.'

'Well, sir, I can ring him at his home and give him that message. Where can he call you back?'

'The Phoenicia Hotel. Room two-four-five. I'll be expecting to hear from him.'

While he waited for the call, he got through to the hall-porter and arranged for a hire-car to be delivered to the hotel as soon as possible. Looking for taxis on a public holiday could cost time and time was something he was getting dangerously low on. The telephone rang out and an almost absurdly bland American voice asked if he were Bob Sullivan and, if so, how he, Walter Masters, could be of service to him.

'I believe you are in Malta for the CIA, Mr Masters. I'd like to talk to you about the Lina Mazzi story.'

'Well, let's start to straighten a few things out, Mr Sullivan,' the smooth voice came right back. 'I am one of two commercial attachés at the United States Embassy. I have no interest in, nor any information to give you about Miss Lina Mazzi. We have a very competent press attaché at the embassy, sir, and I would suggest you channel all inquiries through him. His name is John Everett.'

'All right, Mr Masters—now we've got that out of the way,

let's have another go. My room here at the Phoenicia was turned over last night and I believe you had a hand in it—'

'Now, hold it just there, my fr—'

'You hold it! You can agree to see me straightaway or I start filing a story for my agency that'll produce the kind of headlines your masters in Washington get nightmares about. And I kid you not, Mr Masters.'

If it was a sigh that came over the line, it should have been followed by an indulgent chuckle. There was no chuckle. The voice said, 'I don't want to get in a slanging match with you—it's too pleasant a day. What exactly do you want from me?'

'I want to see what you look like. And I want to talk to you about a gentleman named Burgo. That'll do for openers.'

Masters had found his chuckle. 'Well, Mr Sullivan, I'm beginning to want to see what *you* look like ... Let's see if we can't work something out. My house is in Lija and I'm just on my way to look at some plants in the San Anton gardens. They're about twenty minutes by car from your hotel. Do you want to meet me there?'

'I'm on my way.'

Walter Masters was standing near the duck-pond gazing at a skeletal tree about five feet high with an oversize plaque looped about one of its skinny joints like an identity bracelet on a Belsen inmate. Sullivan had never met him before, and there was already a sprinkling of people taking early enjoyment of the gardens on this public holiday. But this was the only American in sight. He didn't have to have a crew-cut or a camera dangling from his neck; away from his native habitat, the 'Wasp' American was the most easily identifiable of all nature's human species—after the 'Blue' Taureg and the disc-lipped tribeswomen of West Africa. The giveaway was the triumphant eradication of all idiosyncracy in manner, clothing and facial expression. It was *not* the man he had seen with Burgo last evening.

'Walter Masters?'

'Mr Sullivan, I assume.' He did not offer his hand, nor did he smile, unless the slight spasm beneath the lacquered urbanity of his unlined face could be so described. 'A minute earlier and you would have caught me redhanded.'

'Doing what?'

'Filching a cutting from this beautiful thorn-tree—the *chorisia speciosa*.' He gave a little shake of the paper carrier-bag dangling from one well-manicured hand. 'It ought to take very well in my back yard.'

Sullivan said, 'I wish you joy of it. Do the keepers here approve of that sort of thing—or don't you bother to ask?'

'They're decent about it. I use a sharp implement'—he patted the waist of his mohair jacket—'and I only take what I really need.'

'Mr Masters—' They had turned from the flower-bed and were strolling around the pond towards another display of plants on the far side. 'I'm afraid I'm not going to be very decent about the cassette of tape filched from my room last night. I want it back.'

'So would I, in your place. Have you notified the police?'

'I'm short-cutting the procedures. That's why I'm here talking to you.'

Masters stopped to peer at something that looked like a dilapidated lavatory-brush. 'A beauty,' he murmured, plucking a small pair of secateurs from his waistband and squatting down before the plant. And, without looking up from the judicious selection of a shoot: 'I think we might make more headway, Mr Sullivan, if you stopped talking in riddles. What *is* all this about a cassette?' He snipped expertly, slipped the cutting into his carrier-bag and stood up, looking around for pastures new.

'All right,' Sullivan nodded. 'Let's play games.'

'In this direction, it you don't mind.' Masters nodded towards a stone-flagged pathway branching off between some elm trees. 'I'd like to get this little scavenging exercise done while there are not too many people around.' His light blue eyes glanced off Sullivan. 'It's a kind of understanding I have with the custodians of the gardens.'

'Reasonable enough . . . Now here's another little exercise. A young Maltese girl is gang-raped, she says, by three Soviet sailors, and as a direct consequence of this—assuming she identifies the three alleged rapists tomorrow—the Soviet fleet's first visit to Malta is almost certainly going to turn out to be its last. But supposing it can be proved the whole thing was a frame-up, that the so-called Russian sailors were in fact impostors, masquerading as Russians. Do you think anyone's going to have any doubt about who set it up?'

'The question is obviously rhetorical, Mr Sullivan. Why don't you supply the rhetorical answer?'

'I'm working on it. I want you to know I'd be profoundly relieved if the CIA had nothing to do with it. I take the view that a great nation's affairs ought to be conducted on a considerably less squalid level.'

'May I suggest the operative word there is "ought"? One *ought* to be able to walk across New York's Central Park at night without worry, but it's a squalid fact of life that you're more likely to make it home with an acid-sprayer in your pocket.'

'That's pure equivocation. If the CIA is in this, then they're the felons and the Soviet Navy's the law-abiding pedestrian.'

'Let's say the roles are interchangeable—and constantly interchanging. It's only Central Park that stays constant.'

'Like the Mediterranean?'

'Yes, sir. Like the Mediterranean.'

They had reached the end of the path and had turned right, onto a broader walk parallel to the bougainvillaea-covered walls of the Governor's summer palace. Walter Masters was setting the pace at somewhere between an amble and a stroll, pausing occasionally for a brief look at a flowering shrub or to peer upwards into the lofty branches of a tree. With a sense of disappointment, Sullivan now noticed the American had nicked his neck shaving and there was a spot of dried blood on the rim of his white shirt-collar. But perhaps it was not real blood—only a cosmetic device to give an illusion of vulnerability.

He said, 'Tell me, Masters—has it occurred to your people that Lina Mazzi might very easily pick out three Russian sailors who weren't even ashore that night?'

'I imagine it has. As a matter of interest, how would *your* people hope to convince the Maltese they weren't lying about who was and who wasn't ashore that night?'

'*My* people? What the hell is that supposed to mean?'

'The KGB, Mr Sullivan. Don't look so astonished! You've got *me* in the CIA, so the very least I can do is return the compliment.'

'If I thought for a moment you were being serious about that—'

'Why shouldn't I be? The pointers are all there, aren't they? Mysterious cassettes of tape secreted in hotel room. Threats of manufacturing a news-story to get the Soviet navy off this hook they're on right now and discredit the wicked Americans. Let me put it this way— if you're doing all this entirely on your own, Mr Sullivan, I'd just hate to think of the damage you could do with the KGB right in there behind you.'

They had come to an open semi-circle of space with a stepped terrace leading up, left, into the palace; to the right, a glimpse of swans at the far end of a tree-shadowed walk. There was an unreality about the moment—here in the middle of dusty sunbaked Malta—and it was somehow heightened by the two bronze busts on their pedestals, either side of the open area—one of King George V, the other of George VI. Sullivan had been born the day George V died and his mother, a staunch Anglo-Irish monarchist, had fought and won a hard battle with her republican Irish husband to adopt George as the child's middle name. Sixteen years later, Sullivan's Boy Scout troop was subscribing for a requiem mass to the shy successor who had been one of the movement's most devoted patrons. Which was the greater reality—being accused of working for the KGB, or coming across these busts, one of his middle-namesake, the other of a distinguished fellow-Scout, in this semi-tropical garden of a neutralist island? He gave a chuckle and Masters glanced quickly at him and as quickly away, as if offended by the sound.

'I often wonder what it takes,' Sullivan mused, 'to reshape a rational human being into a programmed, imitation computer.'

'You're in a good position to find out,' Masters snapped.

'Seriously, though . . . it's quite inconceivable to you, isn't it, that I could be a non-communist—even an anti-communist—and still be disgusted by practically everything you and your organization have had a hand in over the past twenty years?'

'There's a war on, my friend. It's been on since Vladimir Ilyich Lenin took that journey in a sealed train from Switzerland to Petrograd in April nineteen-hundred-and-seventeen. You can't contract out of it. To be neutral means to be helping one side more than the other, depending on the cicumstances.'

'Get your wars sorted out, Masters. The war you're talking about isn't the ideological conflict that's going to decide the destiny of mankind. That one's being fought *within* nations, not *between* them. The so-called war you want to involve everyone in is the international power-struggle between your country and the Soviet Union. One involves a long-term battle for minds, the other a temporary confrontation of physical power and all the evil and suffering that goes with it. You'll never win the battle for minds with mace, rape and napalm, any more than the Russians could sink the Sixth Fleet with surface-to-surface political pamphlets. This thing you and your lot are involved in isn't a war: it's a state of panic brought on by the fact that you're losing the *real* battle—the one you're incapable of understanding.'

What in hell was he doing here, chopping logic with this chrome-skinned robot? There was a purpose to it somewhere—some subconscious, still-unresolved question clamoring for an answer. They had passed a large greenhouse, and were now drawing abreast of a terrace of high cages. Walter Masters stopped for a moment to stare into the first cage, at a long-snouted primate squatting behind a plaque identifying it as a 'Baboon from South Arabia, Presented by the Royal Sussex Regiment'. The monkey returned Masters' stare, blandly. (*I plead the Fifth Amendment. I refuse to recognise the legality of this court. Go screw yourself.*)

'You're right about one thing, Sullivan,' Masters said, turning away from the cage. 'My "lot", as you put it, isn't in the business of winning people's minds—much as we might

76

pay lipservice to the idea. Our job is to protect the interests of the United States of America wherever and whenever those interests are in jeopardy. We work undercover most of the time and we work to our own rules. And one of these is that America's interests constitute a moral end and therefore justify all available means—moral or immoral—to secure that end. This may shock the pious and irritate our enemies, but that's their problem. So whatever category *you* fit into, Sullivan, you'd better get one thing straight—you're way out of your depth, meddling in this Lina Mazzi affair. The best advice I can give you is to go right back to your hotel, pack your bags and take the next flight out.' He flicked back a cuff to glance at his watch. 'I've really nothing more to say to you.'

'You've said all I needed to hear, Mr Masters. Happy pruning!'

He looked back once on his way out of the gardens. Walter Masters was gazing intently into a cage full of budgerigars.

The entrance to the Hypogeum—a neolithic honeycomb of interconnecting underground chambers—was in Burial Street, an otherwise undistinguished street of terrace houses on the outskirts of Paola. There was only a modest trilithon structure framing the doorway to mark the presence of this 4,500-year-old temple—that and a small marble plaque inscribed 'Hal-Saflieni Prehistoric Museum.'

The crowded central piazza of Paola had been closed to traffic so as to free it for a religious procession and Sullivan had had to be directed through a maze of sideturnings to get to the Hypogeum. There was nobody about on the deserted Burial Street, though a number of cars were parked along the kerb—probably left there by Maltese visiting their relatives for the *festa*. He backed into a free space a few yards from the entrance, then walked up to the door and turned the handle. It was open. He stepped in and closed the door behind him.

There two showcases to the left of the entrance-hall, displaying neolithic objects discovered during the excavations, and a plaster model of some other excavations laid out on a table to the right. The air was cool and still, and though there was no sign or sound of Mr Brecher, the fact of the open front door and the lighting turned on overhead clearly indicated someone was on the premises. As Sullivan walked down the hall to peer over the circular iron rails guarding the descent into a spiral stone stairway, there came a bright flash of light from somewhere below; and when he called out, 'Anyone there?' an answering voice came back, with a faint ripple of echoes in its wake.

'Mr Sullivan? Come on down!'

He counted the steps. At thirty-two they came to an end in a cramped bell-shaped cavern with a low passageway opening on the far side into a large chamber rough-hewn out of the solid rock. There were three steps down to this lower level and the full extent of the chamber became visible only after Sullivan had made the short descent. Towards the centre of the uneven floor a man was squatting behind a camera mounted on a low tripod, squinting at the far wall, whose craggy surface was lit up by a portable battery-lamp to boost the poor illumination from the fixed lighting in the cavern's roof. As Sullivan stepped forward the man looked around and got to his feet. He was about five-foot-ten and adorned with thick-rimmed spectacles and a neat red beard. Sullivan would have put his age at about forty-five.

'Ah, there you are. Mr Sullivan! I was beginning to wonder what had happened to you.'

'These damned traffic diversions ... Am I disturbing you in the middle of a shot?'

'It's perfectly all right. I shall finish it later. You've been down here before, I suppose?'

Sullivan shook his head.

'Well, well! In that case you will permit me to give you a short guided-tour while we talk. I believe I know every inch of the place by now. Quite fascinating in its way.'

'I take it you're an archaeologist?'

'Of no special distinction, I'm afraid. I happen to be compiling an illustrated volume on Mediterranean relics of the copper-age cultures—hence the special permission I have to work here while the place is closed for the *festa*. Malta is quite rich in these prehistoric sites, you know ... Shall I lead the way?'

Sullivan followed Brecher across the chamber, through a low opening and down three more steps into a largish rectangular cavern.

'Nothing of particular interest in the chamber we just came from, except perhaps for that pattern of red ochre traces. It was probably some kind of ante-room to this place here, which some authorities believe to have been the Oracle's room.' Brecher crossed to the left-hand wall, raised a hand to rest in a small oval hole scooped out of the rock and directed an over-the-shoulder grin at Sullivan. 'If you pitch your voice deeply into this hole it reverberates in a quite extraordinary way throughout the upper chambers. One can imagine how impressed an oracle's audience would have been by the sound-effect.'

'Mr Brecher—I don't want to seem boorish, but if I could get just a couple of non-oracular answers to some—'

'I know, I know.' Brecher turned back to him, pulling a face. 'I had been hoping to delay the moment. Actually, there's not a great deal more to show you.' He started back up the steps.

Sullivan called out to him, 'How long have you known Lina Mazzi?'

Brecher crossed the ante-chamber and then on through another low archway, waiting for Sullivan to join him just inside the threshold. A large aperture in the wall to the left opened on a spacious circular cavern decorated with niches and curved cornices shaped out of the vertical rock-face. It was at a level slightly lower than where they were standing.

'The main hall of the Hypogeum,' Brecher murmured. And, turning to face Sullivan, he added, 'Would you believe me if I told you I have never actually met this girl you are talking about?'

'I might,' Sullivan encouraged.

'It's the truth. I will be honest with you, Mr Sullivan. I am one of those men who can only really enjoy sex with girls of—what shall I say?—tender years? Ironical, isn't it, that someone like me, fascinated by ancient monuments like this, should be so aesthetically and sexually switched off by the slightest sign of decay in a woman's appearance? But there it

79

is ... I was given Lina Mazzi's name and telephone number, as a young lady who would indulge this penchant of mine—for a consideration, of course.'

'And so you telephoned her last Monday at the hotel and made a rendezvous?'

'That is correct.'

'Where exactly did you arrange to meet her, Mr Brecher?'

Brecher gave a sad smile and started to reach inside his jacket. In the same moment a woman's voice, huskily scornful, called out from behind Sullivan: 'Let's keep that *our* little secret, shall we?'

He turned around. Mrs Faraclas was standing in a doorway formed by two neolithic pillars and a lintel. She was dressed in what looked like black silk pyjamas, except that the pants were tucked into laced-up leather knee-boots and her hips loosely encircled by a silver-studded belt. Her hands were behind her and she was smiling broadly.

Sullivan spun back to face Brecher, but the bearded archaeologist had stepped to the side, out of line with Mrs Faraclas, and had a revolver pointing like a metal extension of his steady right hand—straight at Sullivan's chest.

5

'It's fully loaded, Sullivan,' Brecher said coldly, 'and you mustn't doubt that I shall kill you if you so much as try to scratch your nose without my consent.'

'Are you both mad? Just what the hell do you think you're playing at?'

'Not newspapermen, today, I'm afraid.' It was Mrs Faraclas, from close behind him. 'Bring your hands back together—slowly. Don't try to turn around.'

He did as he was told, watching Brecher—in vain—for the slightest flicker of inattention. He spoke again as he felt the cold steel encircling his wrists, heard the click of the handcuffs' lock.

'You're insane. I'll have you both behind bars by tonight.'

'In here, if you please,' Brecher said, stepping carefully backwards, down into the circular cavern. As Sullivan hesitated, Mrs Faraclas's boot drove into the small of his back, sending him sprawling through the aperture to roll with the fall and finish up on his back.

'Up!' Brecher motioned with the gun.

He got awkwardy to his feet.

'Bring your legs closer together,' Mrs Faraclas commanded from somewhere low behind him. He made a movement to turn his head, then froze as the gun in Brecher's hand stabbed forward a few menacing inches. There was another click from somewhere between his ankles, then the weight of metal on his insteps. Brecher lowered the gun and nodded to Mrs Faraclas as she walked around Sullivan into view.

'Perfect timing, Maruka. A credit to your old drama teacher. You'd better go up now and lock the street door. Oh, and bring down some of the gear, will you?' He gestured to Sullivan as the Greek ducked through a passageway on the far side of the chamber. 'You can relax now. Let me light you a cigarette.'

The anklecuffs permitted no more than a hobbled shuffle, There were only a few inches of play between his wrists.

'Save your cigarettes for the jail, Brecher—or whatever your real name is. How long do you think you can keep this farce up?'

'Here in the Hypogeum, do you mean? Certainly till dawn tomorrow. We've everything on hand to make ourselves comfortable and the custodians have kindly promised not to disturb us at our—photography.'

'All right—then what?'

Brecher puffed out the match he had put to the cigarette and gave a shrug. 'That gives us time enough to attend to certain pressing matters up above—without interference from you. Then? A sea journey, I would imagine. Romantically. At night. We'll probably take you along as a guest, Sullivan.'

The man was bluffing, of course. But the gun in his hand was certainly for real, and the steel around Sullivan's wrists and ankles wasn't make-believe, and the sudden chill he felt wasn't entirely due to the thinness of his clothing in the cool subterranean temperature.

He said, 'What exactly do you want from me?'

82

'That's Maruka's department.' Brecher backed away to lean against a sturdy wooden rail, beyond which the cavern floor gaped open in a roughly circular well-top. 'Personally, I don't think there's much you can tell us of any consequence that wasn't on that tape you so conveniently recorded for us. But Maruka's convinced you're not working alone—despite the tape's evidence to the contrary. She will want to put some questions to you about that. She has a considerable talent'—Brecher flicked ash from his cigarette —'for getting answers out of people.'

'You're scaring the life out of me. Who does she think I'm working with?'

'Other agents from The Centre, presumably.'

'The KGB!' Sullivan let out a fierce laugh. 'That does it! You're all out of your bloody minds!'

'Maybe ... maybe not. I've checked your overt professional background, of course, and it seems to stand up. But my colleagues are a nasty, suspicious lot, Sullivan. They didn't like the number of visits to the USSR recorded in your passport over the last two years.'

'My job, you stupid bastard! I'm sent there by my agency!'

'Possibly so. The other significant pointer—in my colleagues' view, anyway—is that you haven't paid one visit to the Soviet Embassy since Lina Mazzi made the headlines. The only newspaperman, Sullivan, not to have done so.'

'What's so extraordinary about that, for Pete's sake?'

'Come now, my friend, you don't need me to tell you. The suggestion is that the tom-cat doesn't waste precious time prowling its own back-yard.'

'Brilliant! Which one of you came up with that particular gem of logic? Burgo? Detective Avanzo? Walter Masters?' It was on the tip of his tongue to add 'Daria Safad?' but he stopped in time. The longer they believed the Israeli girl had kept her cover, the better. There was still that matter of three Soviet uniforms ...

'Walter Masters?' Brecher murmured. 'I don't believe I know the gentleman.'

83

'Like hell you don't. Who's putting up the bread for this operation—or are you all in it strictly for the laughs?'

'What's this, George?' Maruka Faraclas came ducking back into the chamber. 'I was under the impression he is here to answer questions, not ask them.'

Brecher shrugged, then raised his gun to cover Sullivan as the Greek crossed the cavern to dump a canvas grip, a folding chair and what appeared to be a rolled-up sleeping bag against the wall. Sullivan watched her unzip the grip, fumble inside and bring out a coil of rope. Without a glance at the other two, she knelt at two small interconnecting holes a few inches apart in the floor of the cavern, a few feet from where Sullivan was standing, and passed one end of the rope through the holes, securing it with a deftly-knotted bowline.

'Maruka got quite excited when I told her about those holes,' Brecher addressed himself conversationally to Sullivan. 'They were almost certainly scooped out there by our neolithic forefathers, probably for the tethering of animals before their sacrificial slaughter.'

'Watch him,' Mrs Faraclas said, working forward on her knees to loop the free end of the rope around the links connecting Sullivan's anklecuffs. She made a slip-knot, tugged it tight, then got to her feet and stood back, thumbs hooked in her belt, to survey her handiwork. 'You can put the gun away now, George,' she muttered. 'It makes me nervous.'

'Just for conversation,' Sullivan said, 'won't your little girls at the Europa be missing you?'

'Still putting the questions?' she smiled, and struck him swiftly and viciously across the mouth with the back of her hand. The shock rather than the force of the blow put him off balance and as he tried to recover it, the anklecuffs toppled him full-length to the floor.

Her boots were snub-toed and highly polished and one of them was only inches from his face. He moved his head to look up at her and, above the foreshortened thighs and jutting breasts, she was still smiling. And he thought, without emotion, *This is when I'll know the bluffing ends—when she puts the boot in*. He rolled quickly away as her hips swivelled, so that the boot thudded into his ribs instead of his stomach, momentarily paralysing him with pain.

'Get up, Sullivan,' she said, 'unless you want the next one in your face.'

He made it to a kneeling position first, then shakily to his feet. Brecher had opened up the folding chair and was sitting against the wall, observing the scene with an air of distaste. Mrs Faraclas was standing as before, thumbs in her belt, just beyond the radius of the rope tethering Sullivan. She was flushed and breathing deeply and her nipples were crisp extrusions through the thin black silk of her shirt. She said, 'We found only one cassette of tape, Sullivan. What did you do with the rest?'

He had to get them worried—whatever the immediate penalty. He said, 'If you mean the cassette devoted to *you*, sweetheart, it's in very safe hands.'

'You are lying. You wouldn't have walked into this trap if you had had any suspicions about me. Or my friend here.'

'Who said I "walked" into it? Have you taken a look upstairs in the street, since I arrived?'

'You are making a mistake, treating me like a half-wit. We have had you followed since you left your hotel this morning. However—' she turned away, walked slowly over to the wall and stood gazing down at the canvas grip—'we know you are not working alone and we want you to tell us all about your associates. We want the truth, and we want to have time to check it's the truth.' She bent down, felt around inside the grip and straightened up. When she turned and walked back to him there was a thin-thonged black leather whip dangling from her right fist.

'You started badly, telling us that stupid lie. Now I'm going to show you what's going to happen to you down here, every time you lie to me.'

With faltering disbelief, he watched her stop a few feet away from him and start to swing the whip slowly back and forth at arm's length, measuring her distance carefully before taking up a stifflegged stance. The flush had gone, leaving her cheeks sallow and intensifying the amber glow of her eyes. Her

85

mouth stayed slack as she swung the whip up behind her, then tightened suddenly with the downward flash of her arm. In the same second a diagonal line of white-hot fire cut through Sullivan's thin shirt from the ball of one shoulder to below his ribs and a half-stifled cry of pain and anger burst out of him.

Her arm was going up again and there was nothing he could do without risking the lash across his face; so he braced himself, clenching his jaws and tilting his head back, and the second stroke brought only a grunt from him, though the agony of it jellied his legs and made him stagger. As Mrs Faraclas, taking unhurried aim, brought the whip whistling down for the third time across the same diagonal of his chest, the shoulder-seam of his shirt sprang open and Sullivan caught a glimpse of scored flesh and bright freckles of blood. Fighting a sudden nausea, he turned awkwardly around as the whip rose again and bowed his head and heard her laughter cut short by a deep grunt as the lash bit into his back.

He took another eight strokes in this position before his legs gave way and he keeled over to the rough stone floor ... There was darkness at first, then an eddying red mist gradually clearing to reveal in soft focus the close-up features of George Brecher. Two strong hands around his biceps pulled him up to a sitting position. He shook his head, blinked at Brecher kneeling beside him, then at Mrs Faraclas, a few paces beyond. The whip lay coiled on the floor at her feet, like a dead adder. She had unbuttoned her shirt and was flapping it with a gentle fanning motion as she stared down at the rivulets of sweat trickling between her bared breasts and down into the hipster waistband of her pants.

'There'll be no more of this,' Brecher said, 'if you'll just tell us what we need to know.' And there was a look of genuine appeal — of sympathy, almost — in his faded blue eyes.

His back felt as if it had been stitched together out of strips of raw flesh. One of his shirt-sleeves seemed to be hanging by a thread from his armpit and his manacled wrists were bracelets of pain. The Greek dike would probably go on working him over, whatever he told them; this was her scene and she was going to play it to whatever limits her kooky needs prescribed. But there was perhaps a slender hope that if he could make

Brecher believe him, and if the 'archaeologist' had any authority over the woman, an idiosyncratic distaste for her methods . . .

He said, 'I work for an international news agency. I am not a KGB agent. There is another cassette, but you'll have to let me out of here before I hand it over.'

Sorrowfully, Brecher shook his head. 'I can't do business with you that way, Sullivan—you must realise that. Mrs Faraclas will eventually get the truth out of you. Why not save yourself a lot of unnecessary suffering by making a clean breast of *everything,* here and now?'

'If I did that, and agreed to take the next plane out of Malta, would you escort me to my hotel and then to the airport?'

'Quite possibly—after I've had time to verify what you tell me.'

Sullivan looked from Brecher's solemn face to the lewdly smiling Mrs Faraclas. It was no good. This was going to be between him and her and there was no way out of it. All he could do was try to delay the torture. 'You'll have to give me more time to think,' he muttered. 'Don't lean on me so hard.'

'All right, George,' Mrs Faraclas said. 'I had better take over again. ' She plucked up the whip and moved closer, flexing the fingers of her right hand. Brecher got to his feet, frowning. 'You're being unnecessarily stubborn, Mr Sullivan. I am going up to make a telephone call. We'll have another talk when I come back.'

In silence, Sullivan watched him go. Then, as Mrs Faraclas circled unhurriedly around him, he doubled back his legs, got to his knees and finally to his feet. He didn't think he could take much more punishment to his raw back without passing out; but as long as he could stay upright he had some measure of choice as to where the lash fell.

The keys to his handcuffs were somewhere on the Greek's person and if only she would come close enough he might be able to butt her unconscious, or at least stun her for the time it took to get his manacles off. He said, with desperate invention, 'Why don't you rip off my shirt? Wouldn't you like to see the damage you're doing with that thing?'

87

But she wasn't buying, 'I certainly would,' she smiled. 'And I have every intention of ripping your shirt off —' She took up a position and, raising the whip, touched the plaited stock to her lips. 'With *this*!'

II

The persistent ringing of the front doorbell brought Daria Safad awake and groping with a sleeplogged arm for the man who had rolled from her spent body what seemed only a few minutes — or was it hours of oblivion? — before. She sat up quickly. There was enough filtered sunlight in the room now to show her she was alone and that Sullivan's clothes were gone from the chair where she had draped them.

The doorbell sounded again — urgent, stabbing buzzes — as she walked stifflegged to the bathroom, wrapped her nakedness in a white mini-kimono and hurried back across the bedroom to pull up the Venetian blinds and lean out of the window.

It was Alfonso Burgo. He was alone, scowling up at her in the warm late-morning sunlight.

'Coming down,' she called to him.

He headed straight for the kitchen when she let him in, and helped himself to a bottle of beer from the refrigerator.

'You should have phoned me first, Burgo, before coming over,' Daria said, following him in. 'Supposing the Irishman had still been here?' Taking a can of orange-juice from the refrigerator she poured some of it into a glass and perched herself on one of the kitchen stools. She looked across at Burgo, then down at her parted thighs and crossed them quickly as the blood rushed to her cheeks.

Burgo said, after another pull at the beer-bottle, 'I don't have to ask you if he gave you a good screwing. You stink of sex.'

'Say what you have to say, Burgo, and then get out.'

He went to the door and looked back at her. 'I'll wait for you in the front room. Go up and put some knickers on.'

She took her time on the bidet and under the shower, brushed out her hair and put on a shirt and slacks. Burgo was standing at the window of the sitting-room when she reappeared. He turned around, let out a grunt and put a match to the cigarette stuck in his mouth.

'We've got to work fast,' he said. 'And no slip-ups this time.'

'There have been only two mistakes so far,' Daria reminded him coldly. 'You made both of them—picking out Lina Mazzi for the rape, and trying to hire that English smuggler.'

'What is done is done,' Burgo snapped. 'It's easy for you to criticise, when all you've had to do is lie on your back with your legs open!'

The Israeli walked to the sofa and sat down. Her lovely face was composed, her blue-grey eyes unclouded. 'Aren't you forgetting a few things? The time I spent winning that little slut's friendship and confidence. The ghastly evenings here, dodging the groping paws of those whoremongers you and Maruka laid on, while I waited for our little star performer to show up. And what about this absurd panic of yours over Bob Sullivan? I take it you were able to search his room—again, thanks to me. How many KGB code-books and sealed orders-of-the-day did you uncover?'

'It's true,' Burgo said thoughtfully. 'I should have listened to you. After all, you've had a lot more experience than I've had in this field.' He whirled on her suddenly, eyeballs rolling. 'And your so-called journalist friend would have led us all straight into Paola Prison!'

She said nothing, but just sat there, motionless, waiting for him to go on.

'We found a cassette of tape on which he had recorded a full account of how I approached Peter Lund and what I asked him to do for us. Then comes a full physical description of me—down to the signet ring on this finger here. There's a neat piece tying in Avanzo with the whole operation, and some bits and pieces of theorising—most of it not so far off the facts. On top of which we found evidence that your Mr Sullivan is almost certainly working for the Reds.'

'What evidence?' she asked sharply.

'His passport. He's been to Moscow seven times in the past two years.'

She said, with a bleak smile, 'He'd be a pretty useless roving correspondent if he hadn't.' Then, with a slight tremor to her voice: 'Was there anything to suggest he knows I'm involved in the operation?'

'Not that we could find anywhere. But Maruka Faraclas is giving him the treatment right now. He'll spill everything before she's done with him.'

The Israeli girl had gone pale. 'You came for him here, I suppose? You were waiting for him earlier this morning, downstairs?'

'We're not that stupid!' Burgo snapped. 'Enough of our covers have been blown, without throwing yours in!' He stubbed out his cigarette and started to prowl about the room. 'What we've got to find out—fast—is who else, if anyone, Sullivan has been working with up to now. I just talked to George Brecher on the phone—'

'Brecher?' Daria cut in.

'Ex-BND. He's in this with Maruka. Great team! They managed to pick off Sullivan between them. He reckons Maruka will get the truth out of the bastard by tonight at the latest.'

'What is she doing to him?' Daria asked in a small flat voice.

Burgo paused in his pacing. 'What difference does it make what she's doing?' he sneered. 'You gave him the last roll in the hay he's ever going to get—in this world anyway.'

She got up from the sofa, walked across the room and, with one slim hand pressed to her stomach, stood gazing out through the window.

'I'd like your attention,' Burgo said.

'You have it. I don't have to *look* at you at the same time.'

'How many times have you spoken to Lina Mazzi since the boys gave her the works?'

'Twice. On Tuesday morning, at police headquarters, and yesterday afternoon, at her home.'

'And you're absolutely sure she doesn't suspect you?'

'Absolutely.'

'Right. Now, you've got to get her here this evening, on one pretext or another. Avanzo will help by calling whoever is on guard at the house to the telephone, at the right time. For obvious reasons, she mustn't let anyone know it's you she's meeting, so you'll have to cook up some clever tale to take care of that angle.' Burgo had been standing still, addressing Daria's back. Now, as she turned slowly around to face him, he resumed his prowling. 'You will get the girl here, sometime this evening after dark. And you'll put some knockout drops I'm going to give you into her drink. That's all. I'll take care of the rest.'

'And what precisely do you mean by "the rest"?'

'I'm going to knock her off—waste her, as our American friends would say.'

Daria was staring at him slackmouthed. She said nothing, only moved to the nearest armchair and sat down as he went on talking.

'These identification-parades tomorrow—they're not going to change anything. A lot of the heat has gone out of the situation since that commie rag, the *Malta Mail*, put out the dirt on Lina Mazzi. All we need now is for her to pick out three Reds who were in the sick-bay or something last Monday night, and the Soviet fleet—and that swine Spitari—will be sitting pretty here for another five years at least. And I'll be back at my old line, flogging blue films to merchantmen crews down at Marsa, instead of buying myself a harem of English crumpet in Chelsea.'

Daria said, 'How can it possibly help us—killing Lina Mazzi?'

'How? We're not very bright this morning, are we, after our night of debauchery?' Burgo stopped in the middle of the room and started methodically to crack the knuckles of one hand. 'If you were a KGB agent, and you had *real* reason to fear Miss Mazzi would identify at least one of the fellows who raped her, by the nail-marks she left on his face or something, what would you most want to do about it—right now?'

'I'd like her to drop dead in her home from some natural cause. I certainly wouldn't try to kill her—that could only swing the Maltese people right back behind Spitari.'

'How do you work that out?'

'Because they'd know for sure, then, the rape was an anti-Soviet frame up and she was killed by the framers, to stop her

91

making a fool and a liar out of herself at the identification-parades.'

'You've got a lot to learn,' Burgo shook his head, grinning. '*You* might draw that conclusion, and so might I. But it's the dumb masses who'll force Spitari to act—and you can fool most of *them* all of the time. Look, I'm going to do that girl in so it looks at first like an accident—until our brilliant police investigators, under the inspired leadership of Detective Avanzo, come up with the evidence that she was in fact murdered—and very brutally, at that. Can't you see the headlines already? Can't you see the mobs that are going to come screaming around the Russian Embassy and the Auberge d'Aragon? I tell you this—if Spitari doesn't immediately cut off from Russia and ban their boats from Malta for all time, *he'll* be the next one to be knocked off— by his own people!'

For a little while she sat quite still, staring past him at some private vision. Then she said, 'I don't like it Burgo. In fact, I don't think I can do what you want me to do without direct orders from the top.'

'What are you talking about? These *are* direct orders.'

'I have only your word for that. I'm sorry, but it's just not enough.'

'Since when? It's been enough all the way along, hasn't it?'

'That was rape. This is murder. It's not that I'm being squeamish, Burgo. I've got to be sure you're not launching out on some maverick course of your own. I need some kind of insurance on this, from higher up.'

'In writing?' Burgo sneered. 'On headed notepaper?' He thrust a hand inside his jacket and brought out a folded oblong of paper. "See what this is?' He opened it up and offered it to Daria's cold gaze. 'Go on—look at the amount written in!'

'Another cheque on a Geneva bank. I'm not in this for the money, you know that.'

'More fool you! But I'm not complaining. Now look at the date. Exactly a week from now—right? Just time enough for written instructions to reach the bank, cancelling this beautiful cheque, if Lina Mazzi isn't taken good care of by the KGB sometime tonight. So, sweetheart—unless you think this is some kind of bonus to us for botching up the rape job, it's all you or any of us can hope for in the way of written instructions.' He thrust the cheque back and took a look at his watch. 'I'll be back some time this afternoon with the knock-out drops. Leave a key under that flowerpot on the porch, if you're out, so I can wait here to go over final details with you.'

He paused on his way to the hallway to look back at her through the open arch of the sitting-room.

'Oh, and if I should see Sullivan—I'll give him your love.'

6

He could see his wristwatch easily enough by bringing his manacled hand round to the side of his waist. He had been in the Hypogeum now for four-and-a-quarter hours and, apart from two further spells of blessed unconsciousness, he had been in pain for the greater part of that time.

It was no longer that outraged protest of shocked flesh that had caused him to scream obscenities at his tormentor after Brecher had left them alone, for the first time, and Mrs Baraclas had again gone to work with the whip. It was now more a throbbing, slow-burning agony, as if his nerve-ends had been so punished they were no longer able to convey acute sensations to his brain, only a dull deep-aching intolerance of the torture.

With Brecher upstairs, she had made good her promise to cut the shirt from his back, circling him like a bear-baiter and snapping the lash so that it hooked and tore away at his thin cotton shirt until it hung in blood-flecked loops from his waist. Only then did she stop, let the whip fall to the floor and, panting for breath, begin to peel off her own damp silk shirt. Her heavy breasts were oiled with sweat and there were protruding little whorls of black hair pasted to the skin at the cleft of her armpits. As Sullivan sank to his knees, she walked over to the canvas grip, took out a bottle of some colourless liquid and tilted it to her lips. Lowering it with a satisfied gasp, she walked slowly back to stand over Sullivan.

'You've been calling me some rather offensive names,' she said. 'Say you are sorry, and I'll give you some of this excellent ouzo.'

Now that the flogging had stopped, a sudden lassitude had come on him, so draining him of strength he could barely raise his bowed head. But he managed it, blinking to focus on her through the ochre haze misting his vision. There were two sets of eyes, mocking down at him—the pair in her face, glinting yellow, and another and lower pair, much wider-spaced: the twin brown stubs of her distended nipples. He said, 'Go and f— yourself!'

'Charming!' She drove the heel of her boot hard into his stomach and took a step back as he keeled slowly over on his side. Then she moved in and began to kick him unhurriedly, between occasional gulps at the bottle still in her hand— aiming the blows where his writhing, rolling body offered a soft target. He was struggling to his knees when her boot thudded into his ribs and a flame of pure pain scorched him from consciousness into oblivion again . . .

When he came to, Mrs Faraclas was lying full-length upon the unrolled sleeping-bag, her head propped against the grip, puffing perfect smoke-rings into the still air. She turned to look at him as, trying to move his legs, he gasped aloud at the pain lancing his left lung.

'Welcome back to the party,' she drawled huskily. 'George won't be joining us for a while. He has gone back upstairs to take a nap.'

He tried to bring his wrist around to look at the watch, but the pain in his ribs checked him.

'What time is it?'

'Lunch time,' she said, sitting up and digging into the grip. 'If you're ready to talk now, I might let you share my goodies.' She unwrapped a package of sandwiches and held one up. 'Smoked salmon and cucumber. I'll feed you myself—after you've told us what we want to know.'

He watched her munching away slowly, her eyes trained expressionlessly on him. There was nothing his racked body wanted less than food, and nothing it craved more than something to drink; and when Mrs Faraclas reached for her ouzo again he must have betrayed this longing, for she made a special production of uncorking the bottle, tilting it with slow reverence to her lips and grunting sensuously as the liquid flowed. He closed his eyes and kept them closed as the Greek's voice came throatily across the floor of the cavern.

'You want a drink, Sullivan?'

He had never been under torture before, but he remembered reading somewhere that a certain stage was reached when a quality of empathy began to invade the relationship between victim and persecutor—a sense of being almost viscerally involved with each other, much as a *matador de toros* was said to be half in love with a brave bull at the moment of truth. Well, that stage hadn't yet been reached so far as he and Maruka Faraclas were concerned. Analysing his feelings towards her at this moment, he was able to isolate anger, frustration and a lust for revenge. There was no sense of empathy or gut-involvement; also, curiously, no hatred and certainly no contempt; one could hardly, after all, feel contempt for someone who quite literally had one's life in her hands. The thought came to him that if he could somehow probe into her mind and learn something of its values, of what made it tick, he might chance upon some fissure in this veneer of objective cruelty, some overlaid vulnerability he might engage, if not for reprieve then at least for a lengthier respite from the torture.

He half-opened his eyes. Mrs Faraclas was now sitting with her back propped against the wall, belt unfastened, legs splayed apart in something like a Yoga *asana*, right hand thrust deep inside the waistband of her pants. Clenching his teeth, Sullivan rolled slowly over and sat up, facing her. She went calmly on doing what she was doing, with the same impersonal regard that took him in as an object, a stimulant perhaps, but denied him all other identity. Her mouth was open, her breathing shallow, audible.

'Having fun?'

'Shut up,' she said.

'I want to talk.'

'You'll talk ... lots of time yet.' She started to breath faster, rolling her head against the wall of the cave; and then she went quite still staring frozenly at him, before snapping her knees together and bowing her head down to meet them. After only a few moments like that she straightened up, reached for the bottle and took several gulps at it.

'You said you wanted to talk?'

'About money. How much do you want to let me out of here?'

Her smile was contemptuous, and for a while it looked as if she wasn't even going to bother to reply. Then: 'You realise we are going to have to do away with you, don't you? There is no way around that.'

'Brecher said there would be, if I talked.'

'And you believed him?' she chuckled.

'If I'm going, anyway, why the hell should I talk?'

'Because if you don't,' she said slowly, 'what I have done to you so far is going to seem like a Bangkok massage. That's why.'

They sat in silence for a minute or so, contemplating each other like a husband and wife poised for a shouting match. Sullivan was thinking, *The bitch seems invulnerable, but she could possibly be encouraged to talk about her 'art'—or 'talent', as Brecher had put it. It might lead me somewhere.*

He said, 'Tell me—were you born like this, or is it something you got hooked on along the way?'

She went on gazing at him for a while. Then: 'You really want to know?'

He nodded.

'I used to beat my young brother, when I was a kid. With a skipping-rope, on his back and legs. He started it—inventing these make-believe situations where I was a cruel

97

princess and he was my slave. I thought it was a pretty silly game at first. Then it began to turn me on, the way it always turned him on, and I started changing the story around.'

Mrs Faraclas took a swig at the ouzo, held on to the bottle for a moment, as if she was about to get up and offer it to Sullivan, then put it down with a shrug. 'Our civil war had been over about two or three years and all the Greek communist leaders were either dead, in jail, or exiled. So I started a new game with Demetrius. He was a Red who had been caught sneaking back into Greece to start another revolution. I was a colonel on General Papago's staff, like my father, and my job was to make Demetrius reveal the names of the other conspirators. But one day—when I was about fourteen, I suppose—I got over-enthusiastic and nearly killed him, and when the story came out about what we had been doing all those years, my father decided to punish me by sending me to a very strict girls' boarding-school in the country.' She let out a harsh laugh. 'Punish me! It was the best thing that could have happened! The headmistress was a lesbian and fell in love with me and between us we had a wonderful time for about two years, thrashing the other girls on the slightest excuse.

'When I was seventeen, the headmistress got me taken on by a drama school in Athens, and from there I went into a repertory company, and it was while I was in Frankfurt with the company, back in 1961, that I met George Brecher. We knew at once we were meant for each other.'

'Wait a minute. You don't mean you two are—'

'Married?' Maruka Faraclas shook her head. 'It was more a marriage of minds—of ideology. George was then working for the West German secret-service, the *Bundesnachrichtendienst*. The BND were looking for a reliable Greek girl to play a part in the plan they were cooking up with the CIA for the murder of Patrice Lumumba, before he could get back to power in the Congo. George took on the job of training me, and after the assassination we worked together in the Middle-East until about two years ago, when the BND dropped us both.'

'Why was that?'

98

'They found out we were making a pile of money on the side, working as mercenaries for the CIA on one or two operations the BND weren't very happy about.' She got to her feet, grinning at Sullivan as she re-buckled her belt. 'Rather similar to this one in Malta, in fact.'

'So I was right about Walter Masters.'

The grin switched to a scowl. 'Don't jump to conclusions,' she snapped. 'I said "similar". I didn't say anything about this Masters—whoever he is.'

'When Peter Lund turned you down, who did you get to rape Lina Mazzi?'

She came over and squatted down, close to him. 'If I told you, what good would it do you?' She wasn't ducking the question; she was closely absorbed at that moment in a study of the weals she had been cutting across his back, shoulders and chest. Here and there—particularly where the lash had crisscrossed over unfleshed bone—the skin had broken and leaked bright trickles of blood that now draped Sullivan's torso like dried, exposed veins. 'You seem to have a high tolerance of the whip,' she murmured thoughtfully. 'Still, I think I'd like to give you some more before trying other techniques.'

Grasping now for fractional extensions of the respite, Sullivan said, 'What can you lose by telling me who did the raping?'

Mrs Faraclas stood up and walked over to where the whip lay beside her discarded shirt, near the wooden rail across the primitive tomb. There were pink indentations in the pale flesh of her back, where it had rested against the rough rock. 'Still playing the newshawk, right to the end?' she mocked, picking up the whip and strolling back across the chamber. 'Well, I'll tell you, Sullivan—but you must promise to keep it to yourself. George got three Hamburg ruffians from a German cargo-ship to do the job. He even saved money on it—the miser—by convincing them they were doing it for the BND. All right? Now—up on your feet!'

It was that or the boot again—and another cracked rib. He managed it and stood facing her, hands clenched tightly behind him.

99

'Here we go again,' said Mrs Faraclas, swinging back her right arm in a full arc.

Four o'clock by his watch, and now the full slow-burning agony as he raised himself on one elbow, torpidly concerned to know why his legs would not respond. The ankle-cuffs were still on, but at some time during his third bout of unconsciousness, Mrs Faraclas had obviously so shortened the rope tethering him to the neolithic eyelets in the floor of the cavern that there were now only a few inches of play in it. She had also removed his canvas creepers, baring his feet. Slowly, as the significance of this act began to register itself, his brain cleared and he raised his eyes, already dreading the confirmation he would find in hers; but she was nowhere in view. He held his breath, listening, and there came to him a sound—faint and distorted—that might have been the sound of voices from somewhere above; but so bizarre were the acoustics in this warren it might also be the echo, still haunting the vaulted roofs, of his last moans as he had sunk gratefully into insensibility... Quickly, he worked his fingers into the back pocket of his chinos and had the cigarette-lighter tightly grasped in one hand when a clumping of boots signalled the return of his tormentor.

She was still shirtless, but the sweat-sheen had gone from her skin, as if she had taken a shower somewhere, and her short blonde hair was no longer tousled. A cigarette glowed between her lips.

She came over, knelt beside his feet and removed the cigarette to give him a crooked, almost defensive smile.

'I never once offered you a cigarette?' she murmured.

'I don't smoke them.'

'Really? So you won't object if I use up a few of them, reciting a sweet little nursery rhyme?'

He said nothing but sat up, bracing himself, as she grasped his right foot low around the instep and used her thumb to prise his big toe and its neighbour apart. The cigarette went to her mouth again and came away red-tipped. 'This little piggy—' she breathed, bringing the cigarette's tip close above Sullivan's parted toes '—went to—' He was telling himself,

100

Not now! Hold it for the second one! when her cry of '*—market!*' was drowned in his own shout of agony as Mrs Faraclas stubbed the cigarette between his toes and squeezed them together.

When she released his foot to light another cigarette, turning a little away from him, he moved a few inches closer, bending his knees and pressing his quivering heels to the floor. She turned back, drawing hard on the fresh cigarette. 'Second line,' she smiled. 'And *this* little piggy—' his foot was seized tightly and the next two toes forced apart '— stayed—'

All the strength he could summon went into his thrusting arms and contracting thighs, and he aimed his brow like a swinging axe to the side of her head where the parietal bone joined the coronal suture, tensing his jaws and neck against the impact and willing himself to stay conscious. There was a grunt from Mrs Faraclas as the lights exploded behind Sullivan's eyes and he stayed, dazed and swaying, on his knees. In slow motion, the Greek's head drooped and she keeled over on her side.

It took almost five minutes' manipulation of the lighter to burn through the rope knotted to his anklecuffs, and at any second he expected to see George Brecher rushing in, alerted by the smell of burning hemp. At last the rope parted. He glanced at Mrs Faraclas, then stood up. She was still out cold. The keys to his manacles were in the breast-pocket of her shirt and he made for it, hobbling across the chamber like a Japanese puppet. What he had to do now was a simple enough gymnastic of stepping backwards over his manacled wrists so as to bring his hands out front, but the pain from his cracked rib and the agonised protest of his lacerated back frustrated his first few attempts. Eventually, clenching his jaws hard, he managed it and found the keys and freed his hands first, unclipping the manacles gingerly from his raw-skinned wrists.

He heard her coming at him as he was crouched over, turning the key in the lock of his anklecuffs, but his reflexes had already taken over, spinning him around and under her tigress leap and then up, with adrenal power behind the thrust of his arms and his shoulders' heave. There was the beginning of a scream from her as she went over the wooden barrier behind Sullivan, but it was cut short by the muffled thud of her skull against the floor of the deep tomb and the brusque sound of her neck snapping.

It took him four seconds to unclip the handcuffs and another two to snatch up the empty bottle over by the sleeping-bag, and he was out of the chamber by the smaller, high-level passageway just as George Brecher came running in from the opposite side.

'Maruka! What the hell's—?' The German took in the discarded manacles and severed rope, then snatched the gun from his belt and advanced slowly towards the exit by which Sullivan had left.

'Maruka! Give me a shout, if you can!'

Sullivan, already at the other end of the passage-way through which Mrs Faraclas had first appeared, could not see Brecher stepping up to the higher level, but he heard the soft footsteps coming nearer and glanced swiftly around for a further line of retreat. There were two exits from the cramped cave he was now in, but no way of knowing which, if either, would lead him back to the Hypogeum's spiral stairway. He went for the larger one, moving noiselessly on his bare feet, and swore silently as he emerged from the rock tunnel into a rectangular chamber, illuminated from the roof and with no break of any kind in the solid walls.

'Sullivan, give it up!' Brecher's echoing voice flowed about the chamber, then sucked itself out like a tidal ebb. 'You haven't a chance!'

Maybe not. But then, again... Two rudimentary pillars, either side of the room's only access, supported a solid rock lintel five feet or so above the ground. There was a foothold in the wall, close enough to one of the pillars to get him chest-high to the lintel, which came out a foot from the wall and offered a good kneeling perch. He had to bite hard against the agony from his ribs as he climbed up, encumbered by the bottle in one hand, and heaved himself onto the rock shelf, but he accomplished it without noise and crouched there, straining his ears for Brecher's approach. The gun should have given the ex-BND man all the confidence he needed, but he was obviously taking no chances. Sullivan could hear him now,

102

halted and breathing softly, somewhere below the lintel—peering, perhaps, to either side of the pillars. He had the bottle firmly grasped by its neck and when Brecher's head inched slowly into view below him he held his breath and raised his arm higher. The head advanced further and suddenly pivotted around, face swinging up, in the same split second that Sullivan struck down with all his might. The neck of the bottle broke off on contact and the sound of the blow was followed immediately by a single explosion from Brecher's gun. Sullivan poised himself to spring, but the German's head, spraying blood, was drooping wearily forward and his body folding in an odd spiral motion towards the floor.

He swung himself to the ground, snatched up the fallen revolver and bent low over the limp body. Brecher's eyes were glassy and his red-bearded lips gaped open, but he was still breathing well enough. It took a long time to drag him by the heels across the outer cave and through the passageway connecting with the 'sacrificial' chamber, and Sullivan had then to ease him down to the lower level by his shoulders to avoid damaging his skull further—and possibly fatally—on the rough rock. He propped Brecher's back against the wall beside the wooden barrier, slipped the revolver in his trouser pocket and leant over the crossbar to peer down into the pit. The body of his tormentor was barely discernable through the gloom. She hadn't moved and from the grotesque angle of her head, never would again.

He turned away and started out for the spiral staircase.

7

The car was still parked where he had left it that morning, with the ignition key under the driver's seat. He knew what he had to do now before he could sit down with a telephone and start dictating his story to the INB teletypists in London; but there was one need more urgent and immediate than any other, and that was to get some liquid into his aching and dehydrated body. Next to that—and, he hoped, not irreconcilable with it—was the need to stay under cover, for to risk being seen now by Burgo, Daria or any other of the gang was to risk ending up with no story except his own obituary notice.

He studied the map of the island provided with his hired car and worked out a route from Paola to Daria's villa that would keep him off most of the main traffic arteries connecting Valletta and Floriana with Sliema and St Julian's—the poles of danger so far as being spotted was concerned. It meant taking a wide circuit to the south of Marsa Racecourse to avoid the harbour area that was Burgo-country, then a full loop bypassing the inland towns of Attard, Lija and Naxxar, and on down through Madliena to the main coast road a mile or so from the turnoff to the Villa Margarita.

He had been driving for five minutes, keeping his eyes on the alert for some modest neighbourhood bar, before he saw what he was looking for, on the outskirts of Qormi. A flamboyant wood-painted sign over the bead-curtained doorway proclaiming it to be the 'Friend to All' Bar. The 'all' included an airborne convention of flies that buzzed him excitedly on his way to the bar—stimulated by the scent of dried blood under his shirt. A boy of about twelve got up from a table spread with well-thumbed comics. There was no-one else in sight.

'Have you any brandy, son?'

The boy tilted his chin, negatively.

Sullivan frowned at the row of bottles along the shelf behind the bar, stepped around and took down a bottle of Hennessy cognac. The boy stared with an impotent awe at him as he upended a glass and poured about three fingers of liquor into it.

'Any beer?'

Another tilt of the chin.

An ancient ice-box stood against the wall by the narrow inner doorway. Sullivan opened it, took out two bottles of Hopleaf and carried them back behind the bar. There was a bottle-opener attached to the counter. He gulped down a tumblerful of the beer, sent the brandy down after it and poured out the second bottle. The boy hadn't budged.

'You don't speak English?'

'Yes. Speak English.'

'What was all *this* about, then?' Sullivan imitated the chin-tilting.

The boy just went on staring at him. He drained the second tumblerful of beer and, turning to replace the brandy bottle, caught a glimpse of his face in the cracked mirror behind the shelf. There was a blue bruise across one cheekbone where Mrs Faraclas's boot had connected and vivid tail-ends of whip-weals

105

curling up out of his collar. He looked back at the boy and forced a grin.

'Car accident,' he said, making the motions of driving, then smacking a fist into his palm. 'How much for the drinks?'

'I ask my father.'

'Don't bother. Here—' he fished a crumpled pound-note from his packet and waved it at the boy '—just give me a dozen or so pennies.'

The lad sidled past him behind the bar and pulled out a drawer. There were a few silver coins and some pennies in a flat tin. Sullivan picked out all the pennies, then a halfcrown, and handed it to the boy.

'For you. Buy some new comics.'

The liquor had put new life into him, but his ribs still hurt like hell and the state of the road after he left the town of Naxxar behind didn't help a bit. At the village of Gharghur he found a telephone box and dialled the *Malta Mail* number. John Carona came on the line, loud and cheerful.

'How's Rome, Bob? And where are you staying— Parco dei Principe?'

'I'm still in Malta, chum. Is Fred Fairchild in the office?'

'Not right now. You'll get him at "Chains" in Spinola Bay, around six o'clock—having a drink there with Ed Summers. What the heck have you been up to, Bob?'

'Busy . . . just busy. I'll fill you in when I see you.'

'Right, but—well, where are you calling from?'

'Sorry, mate. All in good time. Got to go.'

'Bob, hold on a minute! You can't just—' The voice died as Sullivan hung up. He put another three pennies in the box, dialled the Villa Margarita and held the receiver to his ear for a full minute before replacing it.

Five minutes later he brought the car to a stop in the narrow dirt track behind the end wall of Daria's back garden, got out and followed the wall back and around the side of the garden to a low iron gate he had noted as he drove by, after checking there were no cars parked at the front of the house. The gate opened onto a small paved terrace furnished with two brightly upholstered sun-divans and a low glass-topped table. The only way into the house from the terrace was through the french windows of what was obviously Daria's dining-room; and these were locked. Sullivan picked up a small flowerpot, smashed a hole in the pane of glass nearest the inside handle and curled his hand in to unlock the door. He remembered Daria's telling him she had hardly set foot in the dining-room since renting the villa, so with luck his forced entry wouldn't be noticed even if she came back now, before he had finished what he had to do. He was remembering something else: her proposal that they should 'christen' the room—just the two of them—with a candlelit dinner before he left Malta, and his lips had a strained twist to them as he left the dining-room by the door opening on the kitchen end of the hall and made for the stairway.

He had been half-prepared to draw a blank, this time, from the old Maltese chest up on the landing. Daria had obviously had her reasons for not destroying the uniforms three nights ago, after the 'Russian' rapists had changed back into their normal clothes; but now that she knew for sure, from the evidence of the stolen cassette, that Sullivan was on to the plot—if not yet on to her role in it—she must surely be concerned that one of his colleagues might already know where and with whom he had spent last night. But there the uniforms were, exactly as he had replaced them and he took them out and rolled them into a bundle, knotting the sleeves of one of the jackets tightly around it.

And that meant the Big Story was tightly wrapped up as well, and he was ready to split. But not quite yet... He mounted the last flight of stairs and went into the bedroom. Her scent was immediately, subtly, about him. The bed had been loosely remade (maid's day off, for the *festa*?) and a green shirt and a pair of white slacks were draped over the chair where his own clothes had rested. He picked up the shirt and held it to his face, inhaling slowly. If he lived to be a hundred, could he ever forget the smell of her ... ? He put back the shirt, took one more look around the room and started downstairs.

He had reached the foot of the stairway when he heard the sound of a key fumbling into the front door lock, and he made it into the dining-room in one second flat and froze, his back to the wall. The door slammed and heavy male footsteps sounded the length of the hallway, then across the kitchen floor. He eased Brecher's revolver from his pocket and clicked open the safety-catch under the sound of the refrigerator being opened and closed. The footsteps started back the way they had come and Sullivan dived swiftly to new cover beside the arched entrance to the living-room as whoever Daria's visitor was released a loud burp in the next room and flopped heavily back across the sofa. Sullivan laid the bundle of uniforms to rest against the wall and inched his face past the side of the archway. The top of the head visible above the back of the sofa, only a few feet away from him, might have been Burgo's, or any other head dressed with thick black sideburns. But there was no mistaking the hand that appeared now, tilting the beer bottle, with the heavy gold signet ring encircling the second finger.

Long minutes dragged themselves out, and he was on the point of having to make a decision where the greater risk lay—in letting his left leg go completely numb or, by changing position, taking the chance of giving himself away—when Burgo, muttering under his breath, pushed himself to his feet and stumped out into the hallway and up the stairs. Between then and the sound of the lavatory cistern emptying itself, Sullivan had time to slip out through the french windows onto the terrace, stuff the bundle of uniforms under one of the sun-divans and get back to cover inside the dining-room.

Burgo had hardly resettled himself on the sofa when a car door slammed somewhere out front. He was back on his feet, grunting, as the front door opened and Daria's voice came from the hallway.

'Have you been waiting long?'

To Sullivan, crouched in concealment, it was a voice linked to a time indeterminately past, to a delicate mesh of memories already corroding. It was as if the very hours now separating him from that same voice, drowsily murmuring against his chest, had been wrenched out of all emotional perspective and laid to waste. He caught a fleeting whiff of her scent—or perhaps thought he did?—and, as at that moment upstairs when he held her shirt to his face, it offered him now, and would forever, only the bouquet of betrayal . . .

'Long enough,' Burgo's voice answered her. 'I've got to keep moving. Did you fix things with the Mazzi girl?'

'I've just left her. She's going to leave her house at precisely eight-thirty and walk on up to the gates of St Michael's College, where I shall be parked.'

'Good. I'll pass that on to Avanzo ... So that means you'll have her here by around eight forty-five. How can we be sure she won't tell her mother, or anyone else, it's you she's going off to meet?'

'She won't.' The Israeli girl's voice sounded drained, apathetic. 'I told her I had made contact behind the scenes with the Soviet Ambassador, who wants to talk money. Ten thousand pounds for her to pick out three sailors tomorrow who have water-tight alibis for Monday night. Twenty thousand if she publicly admits having invented the rapists' uniforms and nationality. Payment into a Swiss bank and a new start for her abroad. But not a penny if it should get out that I'm acting as intermediary.'

'Nice work.' There was a rustle of paper, then Burgo's voice again, from further away in the room: 'Here are the drops. Empty the lot into her drink. They've got no taste and they'll take about five minutes to work. I'll time it to get here about nine and I'd like her flopped out on one of the beds upstairs when you open that front door to let me in.'

'Upstairs? What's the point of that?'

'I'll give you three guesses.' His voice seeped lubricity.

There was a short silence. Then: 'Don't play games with me, Burgo. Why do you want her upstairs?'

'Let's say it's to spare your maidenly blushes, sweetheart. You're not going to be the only one to get bedroom perks out of this operation. Of course, if it would give you a kick to watch—'

'Listen, Burgo—that girl will be down here, in this room, and you'll put your hands on her only to carry her out of the car. It's that, or these drops go right down the kitchen sink.'

'Cut that out! What difference is it going to make what I do to her? The reds'll be blamed for that, as well as for doing her in.'

'It makes a difference to me! Call me a hypocrite or anything you like, but I mean exactly what I say!'

There was a longer silence, broken finally by a harsh snort from Burgo. 'I've got too much to do to stand here arguing with you. George Brecher will be on that phone pretty soon, to report progress. You know where to get me if there's any new problems.' His voice hardened. 'You're making a big mistake, telling me what I can do and can't do.'

'The only mistake I made was getting involved with an operator like you in the first place. Now I want it over, just so I won't have to set eyes on you again, Burgo.'

'Don't count on it. The world's a small place.'

'Let yourself out. I'm going up to my bathroom, to throw up.'

There came only a grunt from Burgo as Daria's footsteps faded from the room, then his own footsteps as he made for the hallway and the sound of the front door opening and closing behind him.

Moving noiselessly on his canvas sneakers, Sullivan let himself out onto the terrace, then over the side-gate and into cover of the high stone wall. The dust thrown up by Burgo's car was still visible away down the road and he was tempted to follow him, to establish perhaps—beyond further doubt—who was the kingpin and paymaster behind the operation. But that would probably come out in the final wash. Meantime, there were more pressing matters to attend to, and the first of these was to put a call through to Daria, making out it was Brecher on the line. It would be risky, for the Israeli girl presumably knew what the ex-BND agent sounded like; but he felt sure he could reproduce the pitch and the accent well enough to carry conviction over a short telephone conversation. The danger would be in some unpredictable question by Miss Safad, to which he might give a totally wrong answer. Well, he would have to take a chance on that. The greater danger lay in giving Burgo a reason for calling in at the Hypogeum to find out why Brecher hadn't come up to telephone him, as arranged. From what he had just overheard, Daria was going to dope the wretched Lina Mazzi in the Villa Margarita before Burgo took her away somewhere to stage a fatal 'accident',

110

attributable to the Russians. It was a crudely-conceived piece of villainy but it had this going for it: it would work. The Russians could protest their innocence from the rooftops. Political sophisticates might even believe them. Paul Spitari almost certainly would. But the public—with or without incitement from the Nationalists and the Church—would have the Prime Minister's head on a platter if he didn't immediately pitch the Russians out of Malta. This was what Burgo and the rest of his unsavoury gang had been paid to pull off. This was what had put the raw weals on Sullivan's body and burned the tender flesh of his foot. He had a personal account to settle with Burgo and company and he had a story to wrap up. Both these ends would be served when Alfonso Burgo and Daria Safad carried the limp body of Lina Mazzi out of the Villa Margarita, slap into a reception committee of Maltese police . . .

He stopped at a telephone box in a sidestreet of Paceville and dialled Daria's number. Her voice came over the line almost immediately.

'Hallo—yes?'

'Alfonso there?'

'He just left. Is that George?'

'Yes.'

'This is Daria. Did Alfonso tell you— ?'

'Ah, yes. Nothing to report. Everything under control.'

'You mean—'

He made no effort to fill in the pause. She would have to make all the running.

'—nothing has emerged from the inquiry?'

'Nothing yet. We're keeping at it, naturally. Still plenty of time.'

Another silence at the other end of the line—longer this time. Then: 'I've already told Alfonso, I'm convinced we are quite wrong about this. He's quite independent. Quite—unconnected.'

'He has to be connected with *someone*.'

'Not the way you mean.' Her voice had become strained . . . precipitate. 'I know these types. They keep everything to themselves, till they've got it all tied up, don't you understand? All we need do is keep him off the scene until we've—until—' Her voice faltered to a stop.

'Then what?'

For long seconds there was no answer. When she spoke again, the spring had broken and the words limped over the line.

'I'm sure we could do some kind of a deal.'

He couldn't resist it. Still in Brecher's voice, he said, 'You mean *you* could? Between the sheets again?'

'Have you,' the voice came back coldly, 'any other message for Alfonso?'

'That's all. Not to bother about us. Everything under control.' The line went dead.

It had started up again—the bitter, profitless speculation about motives and vulnerabilities and the frontiers of deceit —and he had to wrest his thoughts away from her by concentrating on the next move in the game as he drove on down to Spinola Bay and parked his car across the road from the corner site of Chains, a bar-restaurant John Carona had pointed out to him the day before—*could it really only have been yesterday?*—as they drove past it on the way to the scene of Miss Mazzi's rape. It was now only ten minutes to six. With any luck, Fred Fairchild would show up ahead of Ed Summers and they could drive straight off to a quiet spot somewhere where Sullivan could give him his instructions. But if it was Summers who showed up first . . . He unfolded the map of Malta and held it at the ready, spread across the driving wheel.

Half-an-hour after Sullivan had hung up the telephone on John Carona, Bill Topper was on the line from London, asking Carona if he had had any contact that day with 'our wandering boy.'

'He called me a little while ago, Bill. Wouldn't say where he is, except that he's still on the island.'

'What do you mean—"still"? Where the bloody hell else should he be?'

112

'He was talking yesterday about flying to Rome. And don't yell at me, Bill. I'm a very important man over here.'

'So's a one-eyed man, in the country of the blind— bighead! How's your dolly wife, John?'

'All the better for not having you playing tootsies, like in the Savoy Grill. I heard all about it.'

'If that's all she told you, I'm laughing. Seriously though, didn't Bob leave *any* kind of a trail with you?'

'He was asking for Fred Fairchild. I told him where he could contact him around about this time.'

'Is there a phone there?'

'There's a phone. It's a kind of bar-bistro.'

'Will you get on to Fairchild, John, and tell him that as soon as Bob contacts him to tell him I was asking after him. Just that—asking after him.'

'Right—anything else?'

'You can tell your wife I was asking after her, too.'

Carona hung up, chuckling. He had taken the call from London downstairs in the composing-room, where he had been making some cuts, on the 'stone', in his editorial for the next day's issue: *Confrontation in Grand Harbour*. He returned to the 'stone', told the compositor working at it to let him have a 'dab' of the editorial as soon as possible and hurried back upstairs to put in a call to Chains.

Joe the barman, who took the call, reported only one person in the bar—a foreigner—and asked Carona to hold on while he checked the man's name. A few seconds later another voice came on the line.

'This is Ed Summers of UPI. Can I help you in any way?'

'John Carona here, Ed. We met yesterday at the PM's confernce ... That's right, with Bob Sullivan ... No, I've no idea, but the London office has been on to me, asking for him, and I gather Fred Fairchild is supposed to be meeting you for a drink there, so I—'

'Fairchild's running late, John. You want him to call you, soon as he shows up?'

'Please, Ed. Better still, Bob, who'll probably be popping in to see Fred. Thanks a lot.'

113

Twenty minutes later, an irritated Ed Summers was on the line again to Carona. 'I'm still here at Chains and *neither* of those limey bums has shown up! Have *you* heard from them?'

'Not a peep. Sorry about this, Ed. Are you moving off?'

'I'll give 'em another five minutes. If they haven't called you from here by then, you've lost your messenger-boy, pal.'

'Fair enough. Would you tell the barman to have one of them call me?'

'Right. Anything new on the Mazzi front?'

'All quiet. The calm before the storm. Drop in at the *Mail* any time you're around this way, Ed.'

'I'll do that.'

Ten minutes later, Carona stopped pacing his room and sent for his chief reporter, Charlie Fenech.

'Know what Bob Sullivan looks like?' he asked the thirty-year-old Gozitan as he came through the door. The reporter nodded. 'Well, he's still on the island somewhere and I want him located. Drop everything and take another man with you, in case you have to split up. Who's available?'

'David Arrigo's just back from the regatta. Shouldn't take him more than half-an-hour to knock out his story.'

'Fine. Good driver, young David. Now, this is what I want you to do, Charlie. Get onto the Phoenicia, where Sullivan's been staying, and find out if he's hired a car through them. If he has, check with the garage—make of car, colour, registration number. Then get out there, the two of you, and find that car. You can take my Triumph.'

'What do we do if we find him, John?'

'Not if—*when*.' Carona snatched a cigarette from the box on his desk and put a match to it. 'Don't let him out of your sight, but don't let him know he's being tailed. He's on to something to do with the Lina Mazzi story and wants to keep me in the dark about it. Some angle of his own. I can smell it. I want you to check every move he makes. Don't lose him, Charlie, and report to me on the phone as and when you get the chance. I want you and David to find him and to stay on his tail till I call you off— you got that?'

'Got it, John' Fenech hesitated, turning over a page of the notebook he had brought in with him. Then: 'I think I'm on to a juicy story about some Greek dame who's just taken over as staff manageress at the Europa.'

Carona had started to check a batch of galley-proofs. He looked sharply up, nodding to Fenech to go on.

'I thought I'd better check with one or two of the maids there, in case they could give me any new leads on Lina Mazzi's sex-life. One of them opened up a bit, after I took her out for a drink—well, several drinks, as a matter of fact,' he corrected himself hastily.

'Yes, yes, I'm not querying your exes,' Carona snapped. 'Get on with it, Charlie.'

'Well, it seems this Greek dame's a real butch lesbian, and kinky as hell. Any of the girls who turn up late for work, or are caught idling or anything like that, are given the alternative of either having their money cut or being whacked across the bare ass with a wooden ruler.'

'Why haven't the silly bitches complained to the management?'

'That's just what I wanted to know. According to this girl, Mrs Faraclas seems to be so well in with the manager they're afraid they'll get sacked if they beef about it—and, as you know, there's a lot of unemployment right now in the big tourist hotels. Anyway, the story gets even better . . . It seems that this girl walked into the linen-room last Sunday and caught Lina Mazzi and this Greek woman, well—you know.'

'I do not know. What were they doing, Charlie?'

'Lina was going down to the Greek. Muff-diving.'

'For Pete's sake—don't tell me she's a lesbian on top of everything else!'

'This other maid doesn't think so. She says Lina told her afterwards she wanted the afternoon off and this Mrs Faraclas said she could have it on condition Lina gave her the treatment.'

'Nice work, Charlie . . . Will she sign a statement, your contact?'

'If we can guarantee she won't lose financially by it. I was going to see her again this evening, as a matter of fact, after consulting you about it.'

Carona had pushed the galley-proofs aside to scribble

115

something on his blotter. 'Faraclas...' He spelt it out and Fenech grunted affirmatively. 'Name of your contact?'

'Grace Caleja.'

'Have you talked to the Greek woman?'

'Not yet. She's not on duty today, anyway.'

'Well, don't—for the moment. We have to handle this very carefully, Charlie. Get out and find Bob Sullivan. I'll be doing a bit of a think and we'll talk about this later. Oh incidentally—' he called out as Fenech headed for the door 'how did the Greek take being caught at it by this Caleja girl?'

'Didn't even know she was there,' Fenech grinned back at him. 'Apparently she was having it off at the precise moment the girl put her head around the door.'

8

Fred Fairchild was just two years down from university and owed his job with Intercontinental News Bureaux partly to his blood relationship with one of the company's vice-presidents, partly to the fact that he spoke five European languages fluently and was possessed of a quasiphotographic memory for received facts.

He took no notes as he sat beside Bob Sullivan in the front seat of the car. He nodded his head from time to time and occasionally felt for his right ear-lobe through the thick drape of his strawlike hair and gave it a little tug, as if switching to a fresh cerebral tape.

'... Insist on seeing the Prime Minister in person, and alone,' Sullivan was saying. 'Hold onto the bundle of uniforms and don't let anyone else but Spitari put their hands on it. I don't think there will be any difficulty if you send in your card with the note from me written on the back. Above all, do not

117

discuss what I'm going to tell you now with anyone—I mean *anyone*—except Spitari.

'I want you to tell him that I now have most of the evidence lined up to show that the gang-raping of Lina Mazzi was carried out not by Russian sailors but by three German seamen paid to do the job, wearing these uniforms, by a fellow called Alfonso Burgo who is almost certainly involved in some kind of deal with the CIA. I can't prove, right now, that the CIA is behind it and there's no time for me to dig deeper into this side of things because Miss Mazzi is going to be murdered tonight by this same Burgo and his accomplices unless Spitari acts the way I want him to on this information.

'At eight-thirty sharp this evening, Lina Mazzi is going to leave her home for a rendezvous with an Israeli girl called Daria Safad who is a key figure in the conspiracy and who was responsible for luring Lina into the rape area last Monday. In no circumstances is the girl to be prevented from keeping this rendezvous, and no attempt should be made to tail her or the Israeli. These people are not stupid. If Spitari wants to catch them redhanded this time, he must follow my instructions to the letter.

'Now, listen carefully to this, young Fred ... Tell the Prime Minister to send a couple of his security men to the Hal-Safliena Hypogeum, as soon as he likes, to pick up a German gentleman called George Brecher, whom they'll find manacled to a wooden post in one of the underground chambers. Brecher is in the plot and I've got the dope the authorities will need on him. In a nearby pit they'll find the body of a certain Mrs Maruka Faraclas, late of the Europa Hotel. Her death was accidental but I can't pretend I didn't contribute to the accident and if you could see what I look like under this shirt you would understand why.'

'Is that where you collected this, too, Bob?' Fairchild pointed to his cheekbone.

'That's only the half of it, mate. The bitch would have been an asset to any of the South American soccer teams ... Now, get this: no word about any of this—the uniforms, the Hypogeum, the rendezvous between Lina Mazzi and Daria

118

Safad—must leak to a certain Detective-Inspector Avanzo, unless Spitari wants the whole operation blown sky-high. But nor should any move be made against him—yet. Daria Safad will drive Lina Mazzi to the Villa Margarita, arriving there around eight-forty-five.' Sullivan handed Fairchild a piece of paper. 'Here's a map of the villa's location. Shortly after that, Alfonso Burgo will show up and wait out front somewhere till Safad lets him in. She'll do this as soon as Lina has taken some knock-out drops and passed out.

'If Spitari can arrange with the Commissioner of Police— who obviously will have to be taken into his confidence—to have armed policemen set up a road block here—' he pointed to an X marked on the pencilled map '—Alfonso Burgo and anyone else he might have with him will drive right into it, probably just after nine o'clock. And the Mazzi girl will be with them—unconscious. That's assuming the cops don't blow it by showing themselves on the scene before eight-forty-five. I shall be hidden inside the house, to keep tabs on Miss Safad, who almost certainly will not be leaving with Burgo ... All right, Fred—any questions?'

'Just one. Why stick your neck out, Bob? Why not just tell Spitari everything you know and leave it to him and the fuzz to do the necessary?'

'For two good reasons. I want to be in there right at the kill so I can wrap up my story and put it straight over the wire. And I have a couple of personal matters to discuss with Miss Safad before she's made an incomunicado guest of the Maltese Government. Anything else?'

'You got a gun?'

'I borrowed Brecher's.' Sullivan tapped his trouser pocket.

'Great. Well, I'd better get those uniforms out and start looking for a cab.'

'Just one thing. I'm starving all of a sudden and I'm out of cash. Give me a couple of pounds and I'll find some off-beat joint where I can fuel up for the last lap.'

'Do I get an IOU?'

'Yes, mate. Right up yours.'

He had parked his car outside a sleazy-looking bar restaurant in a sidestreet of Paceville and was about to climb out when he heard a screech of tyres from somewhere behind. He glanced at his rear mirror, then ducked quickly down. Thirty or so yards back at the intersection with the main St Julian's Road, a red Cortina—the same model as Daria's—had braked to avoid hitting a jay-walker. There was a girl at the wheel. He didn't need to take another look at her. He stayed down until he heard her drive on, then got out and walked into the bar.

His watch showed exactly a quarter to seven. It meant Miss Safad still had an hour and three-quarters to get to her rendezvous outside St Michael's College—a bare five minutes' drive away. Obviously, she had other matters to attend to before meeting Lina Mazzi, and this could turn out to be a good break for him. If he rushed his meal he could have plenty of time alone in the Villa Margarita to give the place a going-over for any other secrets it might still have to yield.

The menu—passed over to him by a middle-aged English couple sitting at the only other table laid for eating—offered him a choice of steak and chips, fish and chips or *cannellone* and chips. The Englishman, catching his eye as he looked up from the menu, removed the pipe from his mouth and gave Sullivan a compatriotic nod.

'I'd go for the steak, if I was you, old chap. The fish is frozen and that cannellone—' he raised a cupped hand to his mouth and dropped his voice '—well, it's a rissole wrapped up in stale putty, no joking.'

'My hubby's right,' his companion put in, making a face. 'We always go for the steak, don't we, Bert. At least you know what you're putting inside you.'

'Thanks for the advice. I—er—' he peered past them, towards the open doorway leading to the kitchen '—I'm in a bit of a rush.'

'Tony'll be out in a minute,' the man said. 'Here on holiday, then, are you?'

'Just a trip.' He was staring at a copy of the London *Daily Express*, folded under the man's elbow. The overseas papers hadn't yet arrived at the hotel when he had set out for his meeting with Masters that morning. 'Would you mind if I took a quick glance at your newspaper?'

'Help yourself, friend,' the man said, passing the newspaper over.

Bill Topper hadn't been kidding. The Mazzi story was holding its own on page one against all international and domestic competition. A banner headline proclaimed:

SOVIET NAVY'S BIG GAMBLE. And below that, across four columns : LINA TO IDENTIFY RAPISTS : SPITARI CALLS FOR RESTRAINT.

Sullivan quickly scanned the first few paragraphs.

In his promised TV appearance last night Malta's neutralist Prime Minister, Mr Paul Spitari, told the island's outraged population that the Commander of the Soviet naval force, at present sharing harbour facilities with units of the US Sixth Fleet, had agreed to stage identification parades tomorrow aboard the Soviet ships under his command.

First reactions in Washington to this surprise turn-about in the Soviet attitude were cynical. Said a spokes-man for the Defence Secretary: 'It's asking a great deal, after a five-day delay, to expect anyone to make positive identification of three faces out of so many hundreds. The Soviet authorities' refusal on Tuesday to extend immediate cooperation to the Maltese police must put in question the sincerity of the motives behind this *volte face*.'

He looked up from the newspaper as the chef-cum-barman-cum-proprietor appeared through the doorway, wiping his hands on a dishcloth.

'Nice steak-and-chips for our friend here, Tony,' the Englishman piped up from the next table. 'And he's in a hurry.'

Sullivan handed back the paper as Tony gave a grunt and returned to the kitchen.

121

'Proper muck-up they're making of the rape affair,' the Englishman snorted, dropping the paper under his seat. 'I reckon old Spitari's hand-in-glove with those Russians, if you ask me.'

''Course he is,' the wife said, shooing a fly from her empty teacup. 'He invited them here in the first place, didn't he?'

'Nasty knock you got there, old chap.' The husband brushed his cheek with the stem of his pipe. 'Dive in a swimming-pool after they let the water out, did you?' He grinned at his wife, who had let out a shriek of laughter. 'We shouldn't laugh about it, by rights. Other people's misfortunes...'

Sullivan said, 'I got mugged up in The Gut last night. Took all my money, they did.' He had their uneasy attention and he held it with a plaintive, desperate stare. 'I was wondering—I don't suppose you could help me out with the loan of a fiver? I'd let you have it back, of course.'

It worked perfectly. He saw the woman's hand dart under the table to pinch her husband's thigh, watched the sudden dissolve of that worthy's bonhomie into furtive embarrassment.

'Wish we could, old chap... Matter of fact, we're a bit pressed ourselves. Near the end of the holiday, you know how it is.'

'Time we was getting along, Bert,' the woman muttered, reaching down for her handbag. 'We've got these friends waiting for us, you see,' she grimaced at Sullivan.

'Even just a couple of quid would be a help,' he wheedled. 'I could give you a cheque.'

'Yes—well, as I was saying, Bert—we've got these friends waiting up the road.' She didn't even wait while her husband hastened into the kitchen to pay his bill, but made straight for the street exit, clutching her handbag tightly to her bosom.

'Even five bob—' Sullivan whined as the man came hurrying after her. 'I'm not proud.'

The fly-curtain swirled violently in hubby's wake.

Sullivan, grinning, reached down for the abandoned newspaper and opened it up again to check the rest of the

122

news. His eye was caught by the heading on a short item down-page in column six.

BRITON DIES IN MAFIA
SMUGGLING VENDETTA
The converted motor-torpedo-boat, *Gurkha* ...

He closed his eyes. *Oh, no — not Lund! Let it not be Peter Lund.*
He read on, his stomach knotting hard.

... believed to have been 'muscling-in' on the Mafia-controlled smuggling of cigarettes in the Mediterranean, was destroyed by an explosion in the harbour of Tunis last night. Mr Peter Lund, the Guernsey-born owner, and three of the crew — all Spaniards — perished in the explosion. The rest of the crew, including an unnamed Englishman, who were ashore at the time are being detained by the Tunisian police for questioning.

Sullivan sat perfectly still, staring sightlessly at the opposite wall. He was remembering Lund's words: 'Might as well tell you the story. I can't see it doing me any harm, anyway, since I shan't be putting back to Malta — 'cept maybe on some luxury cruise liner.' It mattered now to Sullivan, and it would matter all his life, that he accepted the possibility it was in fact the Mafia who killed Lund; because, if it wasn't the Mafia, it was *he* who had promoted the killing by recording Lund's testimony on that cassette ... A cold anger usurped his guilt. It didn't matter any more if Lund's evidence against Burgo and Avanzo had been made inadmissible through his death. What mattered was the residual possibility — hell, the near certainty — that his murder had been the tribute exacted for something a lot more important than a cargo of contraband cigarettes, and that the animals mainly responsible for it were still at large.

He had telephoned the Villa Margarita once while Tony, the assassin of good meat, had been making out his bill. Now,

123

from a garage at the start of the coast road, he called the number again, and again there was no answer. Nevertheless, this was not the stage of the game for taking chances and so, as he neared the point along the dirt road where the villa was about to come into view, he stopped the car, got out and made a quick reconnaissance. There was no sign of life anywhere about the house. No car in sight. He drove on, took the track around to the rear of the garden and parked where he had parked before.

The flowerpot he had used on the french windows was exactly where he had left it and fragments of broken glass were still on the floor, just inside the dining-room. He stepped in, leaving the door ajar, and paused for a moment, trying to make up his mind where to begin the search. He would need to be in a front room as eight-thirty came around, with his ears pricked for the sound of Daria's car. He had better start in the kitchen, then back to the dining-room and on up to the guest-room on the floor above. But, first, a quick glance around the living-room.

As he started to pass through the archway, the voice of George Brecher said, 'I'm exceedingly annoyed with you, Mr Sullivan,' and he froze. The words had come from over to the left, and Sullivan turned his head slowly and there was the German, lying back in an armchair, his pale blue eyes blinking reproachfully from beneath the gauze field-dressing taped across his brow. Even as Sullivan's hand flashed in and out of his trouser-pocket he realised he had been jumped and he froze again, with a silent curse, as Burgo's voice snapped at him from the hallway.

'Hold it—*just—like—that!*'

Brecher stayed where he was, balefully watching as Burgo, gun in hand, moved up behind Sullivan and relieved him of Brecher's revolver.

'And you still,' Burgo ground out, 'say you're not working for the KGB?'

Sullivan stayed silent. The shock of seeing Brecher again had been bad enough: the realisation, now, that he was in the hands of two men who hadn't one good reason between them for keeping him alive and every reason for knocking him off was for the moment jamming his thoughts with strident oscillations of fear.

'You kill one of our people,' Burgo ground on. 'You escape from my friend here but do *not* go to the police and tell them all about it. Instead, you phone our Israeli associate, making out you are Brecher here, and thereby proving you were here earlier, eavesdropping on my conversation with Miss Safad. Oh, you're a smart fellow, Sullivan. You took Daria in, all right. Your mistake was in not covering the possibility I might just decide to look in at the Hypogeum to ask you a couple of questions myself.' He drew a slow breath. 'I'm going to ask you some now. Why did you come back here? And what else have you been up to since you got away from the Hypogeum?'

'Cooking your goose, Burgo,' Sullivan said. 'It makes no difference whether you think I'm KGB or a genuine newsagency man. Either way, you don't think I'd walk back here without first setting it up for the whole lot of you to be nabbed?'

Burgo was manipulating a cigarette and a lighter with his free hand. He drew hard and exhaled. 'What do you think, George?' he muttered.

'If he were KGB he'd have phoned his people at the embassy and they'd have told him to pull right out and let the Maltese authorities take over. There's no other way they'd play it, you can take that from me. I think this fellow is probably just what he says he is. But he also wants to be a hero. He had my gun. All he thought he had to do was wait here for Daria, you and the Mazzi girl, then hold you all up while he called the police. By-passing Detective Inspector Avanzo, of course.'

'Could be,' Burgo nodded. 'I'd still like to know exactly what he's been doing with his time.'

Sullivan said, 'If you're all that interested, I'll tell you. I've been eating a leathery steak and chips in Paceville. But before that I had a long chat with a colleague who just about now is with Paul Spitari. So you see, you're both going to wind up in jail for a good stretch. If you kill me, you'll go in for life.'

Brecher pushed himself up from his chair and walked over to the drinks-trolley. 'You're not so smart, Sullivan, after all. You've just given us the best reason there is for putting you away. Look at it. Another cassette of tape somewhere—so you say—with unverifiable evidence against us . . . Your colleague's purely hearsay evidence . . . A dead Greek woman, somewhere. A dead Englishman—you—somewhere else. And a nastily-murdered Lina Mazzi. What does it all add up to? With you around to testify—plenty. Without you—utter confusion. In fact, just the sort of confusion a classic KGB operation would try to create around the death of Lina Mazzi. I'm just sorry Burgo and I won't be around to add to it.' He slowly drained a jigger of cognac, wincing slightly as he tilted his head.

It had to be said. He had wanted to keep it back, without quite knowing why; but there was no way of doing this now—and staying alive. He said, 'You're forgetting something —the phony Russian sailor uniforms. I found them here and gave them to my colleague to hand over to Spitari.'

Burgo's expression did not change. He kept the gun and his eyes trained on Sullivan, seemingly waiting for his colleague to say something. Brecher, who had been staring intently at his wristwatch as if into a miniature crystal ball, gave a shrug. 'Let's go,' he muttered. 'We've already wasted enough time here.'

Wherever they were going, they were taking no chances on Sullivan's pulling anything en route. They marched him at the points of two guns out through the back terrace and around the wall to the place where he had parked his car. Here, Burgo ordered him into the driver's seat and kept him covered while Brecher climbed into the back. Then Burgo took his place up front beside Sullivan.

'All right. Get going.'

He swung left, as ordered, when they reached the sea road, and they drove on in silence, following the coast's contours for seven or eight miles as far as a bay wide open to the sea but tapering inshore, as they drove around it, into saltflats overlooked by a modernistic pile of concrete and sandstone proclaiming itself the Salina Bay Hotel. A road sign indicated

St Paul's Bay somewhere ahead, but at Burgo's terse command Sullivan slowed down at the next crossroads and turned left, climbing up inland along a winding secondary road signposted 'Bur Marrad'.

He was making a careful note of landmarks as he drove. At the same time his mind whirred with speculation as to his captors' intentions now that he had shot down their earlier plans. Clearly there was going to be no rendezvous now between Burgo and Daria at the Villa Margarita. Burgo must have telephoned her as soon as he had got Brecher out of the Hypogeum, heard about the telephone call from the other 'Brecher' and immediately cancelled the existing arrangements for the murder of Lina Mazzi. But did this mean they were not going ahead with it some other way? With the cassette of tape destroyed, with Peter Lund dead and he himself obviously marked for the same end, what was left on the chessboard to give the conspirators any grave pause? If Sullivan was a KGB man using a newsagency cover, the Soviet Embassy in Malta would have been fully briefed by him and might indeed have invited the police to lay a trap that evening at the Villa Margarita. But when no one turned up? When the corpse of Lina Mazzi was discovered later, a few hours before she was due to identify her Soviet rapists? Would anyone seriously doubt that the Soviet 'tip-off' to the authorities was anything but a clumsy last attempt to throw the guilt for Lina's murder on the CIA agents who had staged her rape and who were now 'panic-stricken' she was to botch up everything by fingering three certified homosexuals, or something, aboard the Soviet ships?

Taking the other tack, and if they decided Sullivan was no more nor less than what he claimed to be—again, where was the danger to Burgo and company? His own murder could as readily be attributed to the KGB as to the CIA—more readily, in fact, given his presumed loyalties and Western democratic background. (*There was clear physical evidence, the police state, of his having been tortured before being done to death.*) The average Maltese would never accept that the American CIA could indulge in or condone torture. They had been protected too long by an uncritical, pro-American press and TV service from harsh truths about the CIA known to every American schoolboy. What about Maruka Faraclas—or whatever her real name was? They would already have removed her corpse from the Hypogeum to avoid incriminating the 'archaeologist' George Brecher. Her disappearance from the Hotel Europa could only fuel the case against the KGB—particularly when it was 'leaked' that this friend of, and mourner for, Lina Mazzi was a former BND agent and a trusted CIA contact. The irony, of course, was in the fact that the paw-marks of the CIA these days were virtually indistinguishable from those of the KGB wherever villainy was being perpetrated. One remembered how, in one's youth, the image of the British and American secret services was heroic and, on the whole, *decent*; only Stalin's NKVD was abominable. All that had changed, so far as the US was concerned, with the rise to power in 1953 of John Foster Dulles, the apostle of 'brinkmanship', when that severe Christian missionary gave his brother Allen at the CIA the green light to match villainy with blacker villainy in the contested areas of power-politics. Between them, the two Dulleses had effectively blurred all moral contrasts between the US and the USSR in the nefarious protection of their respective interests abroad. In most instances this was now working to the CIA's disadvantage and accumulating discredit. Here on this politically still-unsophisticated island, in the case of Lina Mazzi, it could work to their advantage.

Sullivan's captors hadn't reacted as he had hoped they would to his revelation about the Soviet uniforms. Whether they believed him, or had dismissed his story as a bluff, there was an unexplained factor here that had been nagging at Sullivan since he had first laid eyes on the uniforms in that antique chest at the Villa Margarita. Spitari, however, would certainly leap at their significance as evidence—as he would readily accept, until discredited, the account of Sullivan's activities as relayed to him by Fred Fairchild. But unless the Prime Minister ignored his request not to put a police tail on

Daria Safad at St Michael's College—assuming she was still keeping the rendezvous with Lina Mazzi—there was no salvation for Sullivan in that direction—any more than that the uniforms, in themselves, would save Spitari and his neutralist policy from the public fury to be unleashed by Lina's murder. Daria Safad, *bona fide* Israeli State employee, would laugh Fairchild's story off as the purest fantasy. 'Find the Russians who dumped those incriminating uniforms,' it would be said, 'and you'll find the beasts who raped Lina Mazzi.'

His thoughts were converging again on his own plight. He had little chance of making a fight for it—and surviving—so long as two guns were trained on him; but a moment would surely come, after that had reached whatever was their destination, when there would be only one gun on him—and that was when he would make his break. He wasn't going to die like the resigned victim of some Cosa Nostra 'soldier' or the petrified prey of some young American psychopath. A revolver was a singularly inaccurate and unreliable device for delivering lead into a fast-moving target. Provided he still had his hands free when the opportunity came ... Hell, even if they weren't! He desperately did not want to die, but if he *had* to he'd be damned if he made it a pushover for them.

'Turn down here,' said Burgo as they reached a fork in the winding stone-hedged lane they had been following since branching off the Bur Marrad road to traverse a bleak scrub-covered ridge. Twenty yards down the bumpy dirt road two crumbling sandstone pillars marked the entrance to a derelict driveway up to what looked in the gathering dusk like an abandoned old farmhouse.

'Stop the car by the front door there. Then stay seated with your hands on the wheel till I tell you to get out—unless you'd rather Brecher blew the back of your head off right here.'

Charlie Fenech, chief reporter of the *Malta Mail*, had telephoned the Phoenicia Hotel a few minutes after seven and had been given the name of the car-hire firm servicing Bob

Sullivan. He put a call through to them at once and a minute later was scribbling the details on his desk-pad.

White Ford Anglia saloon. 1971 model.

Registration number: 55674.

'White!' he sighed, hanging up. 'Why couldn't it be candy-striped? Or a convertible? Or anything but a bloody Ford-Anglia?' He called over to David Arrigo, stabbing away at a typewriter on the other side of the room.

'How's it coming, David?'

'Like congealed tapioca.' Arrigo flicked a long switch of hair back from his brow and reached for a fresh cigarette. His English was quite accent-free—one of the gifts of Stonyhurst College in Lancashire. 'Another quarter-of-an-hour should see it off, Charlie.'

'Scrub the fancy prose and make it seven minutes. This job's a Carona priority.'

Twelve minutes later, as Arrigo gunned the Editor's Triumph Spitfire out of the car park of the ruined Opera House and headed out of Kingsway, Fenech filled him in on what they had to do.

'White Ford Anglia!' Arrigo echoed Fenech's disgust. 'The island's crawling with 'em! We just passed three of the bastards!'

'So all right. We're looking for five-five-six-seven-four. Question is—how do we section-up the search?'

'Didn't the Editor give you any briefing about where we should concentrate?'

'He hasn't any more idea than we have. I suggest we start with a wide coastal sweep, taking the car-parks of every hotel from the Phoenicia to the Sheraton at Paceville, then up inland to Rabat, Mdina and the Corinthia Palace at San Anton, then on down to St Paul's Bay: If we haven't spotted him by then, we'll have another think. Oh yes, and John wants us to check that villa where the Israeli-wine bird lives. Apparently she and Sullivan have been having it off together.'

'What's he got I wish I had, dammit?'

'The fact that he's an in-and-out visiting fireman who can't hang chains on her, I suppose. So cut out the day-dreams and keep your eyes skinned, okay?'

Arrigo drove fast and resourcefully, exploiting most of the eccentricities of the other road-users to his own advantage. It meant that on the few straight stretches between Floriana and Paceville he zigzagged the lanes like a *slalom*-skier and that he overtook on the blind curves, leaning on his horn and the hope that whoever was coming the other way wouldn't be panicked into doing anything reckless—like holding to his course. But a dozen diversions to inspect hotel car-parks piled on the minutes and by the time they finally reached the dirt road leading to the Villa Margarita it was already gone nine pm. There was no sign of a white Anglia anywhere near the villa or its surrounding slopes, or of any other life—until they turned back and were rounding the bend of the road running back down to the coast. A police-car blocked their way and as they braked to a dusty stop two khaki-uniformed sergeants and three constables stepped from cover either side of the narrow road. The constables carried carbines. The sergeants had their hands resting on opened holsters. The Triumph's two doors were swung open.

'Out—both of you!' snapped the older sergeant.

'What's all this, Mike?' Fenech leaped out, grinning. 'Don't tell me the revolution's started already!'

'Key to the boot,' the sergeant grunted. He watched, grim-faced, as David Arrigo reached back inside the car, groped about the facia and brought his hand out dangling a bunch of keys.

'Haven't the faintest idea which one it is, Sergeant. It's our Editor's car, you see.'

The sergeant obviously disapproved of longhaired young compatriots with languid English public-school voices.

'Open up!' he barked in Maltese.

'Here, I'll do it.' Fenech took the keys from Arrigo and walked around to the boot, with the senior sergeant close behind him. 'What are you looking for, Mike? Hash? Porno?' He raised the lid of the boot and stood aside while the sergeant probed around the spare wheel, opened up the tool kit and gave the empty petrol-can a few shakes.

'All right, you can lock it up again.' The sergeant waved the

131

three constables back into cover and nodded to the other sergeant, who slipped smartly behind the wheel of the police car and started to back it off the road and into the walled courtyard of a villa still under construction.

'What are you two doing up here?' He was shepherding the reporters back into their car as he put the question.

'We're trying to track down an English colleague, name of Sullivan,' Fenech said.

'What do you want with him?'

'It's not what I want with him, Mike. It's what the Editor wants. Don't tell me you're looking for him, too.'

'I don't want you hanging around here, Charlie.' The sergeant had the car door open and was frowning at his wristwatch. 'Get in and just keep going.'

'All geared up with guns—yet!' Fenech was shaking his head, taking his time joining Arrigo on the front seat. 'There's the smell of a good story somewhere here, David my boy.'

'No doubt of it,' Arrigo said loudly. 'What a pity the sergeant won't give us a break.'

'Very impressive photo we happen to have of him in the picture-library,' Fenech sighed. 'Without the gun, of course.'

'Move!' barked the sergeant. 'If you're within a mile of here in three minutes' time, you'll both spend the night in a cell!'

Arrigo, chuckling, put the car into gear and gunned it off to a racing start, leaving the sergeant backing out of a cloud of dust.

'Get to a phone-box,' Fenech muttered as they broncho-ed on down to the coast road. 'I'd better have a word with John about this.'

They pulled in at the garage where, two hours earlier, Bob Sullivan had made his last call to the Villa Margarita before walking into Burgo's trap; and while Arrigo kept the pump-attendant outside, filling the Spitfire's tank and checking the oil, Fenech got through to Carona and reported what they had just seen. The Editor heard him out without interruption. Then: 'What makes you so sure Sullivan wasn't already inside the Israeli bird's villa, Charlie?'

'There was no sign of his car anywhere. I'll go back if you

132

like, but Sergeant Agius didn't seem to be kidding about running David and me into jail.'

'You'd better keep out of it then. Stick around somewhere on the coast road, near the turn-off to the villa, till I get another man down there, fast. He can take up observation, leaving you and Arrigo to carry on looking for that car. Check back with me here from time to time, whenever you get the chance.'

9

Bob Sullivan was sitting in a recess shaped out of the bare wall of the kitchen of an old farmhouse below the Wardija Ridge. They hadn't tied him up. They were watching him from across the other side of the room, at a firing range of about ten yards—Brecher perched on an upturned crate, Burgo standing by the paneless window cut into the two-foot thick walls.

'Time for you to get moving, George,' the Maltese grunted, breaking a long silence. 'I'd go myself, if it didn't mean leaving you here alone with this crafty bastard.'

'I'm all right.' Brecher pushed himself to his feet. Against the pallor of his face the German's neat beard offered a stark henna-ed contrast. Dyed? Sullivan wondered as he tensed his legs hopefully. Why not? It would be a minor detail of this one's protective camouflage.

They weren't giving him so much as the blink of a chance.

Brecher was backing towards the doorway, his gun still trained on Sullivan. And they went on talking without looking at each other, as if each word was being addressed directly to him.

'How will I recognise her?'

'She'll be driving a red Cortina and she'll have the Mazzi girl up front with her. She'll stop the car on the main road, alongside the Kennedy Memorial, and flick her headlights every five seconds till you give her three quick pips on the horn. All you have to do then is lead her in.'

'Good enough. What signal will she give me if she knows she's been followed?'

'No signal. She won't stop, she'll just drive straight on. Oh, and George—' he stopped Brecher in the act of backing out of sight '—one long blast on the horn as you come up to the fork down the road there. I'll be listening for it.'

Burgo stayed where he was, eyes fixed on Sullivan, listening to the sounds from the driveway as Brecher opened and closed the car door, started up the engine and engaged the gears. When there was nothing more to be heard but the distant hum of the motor, he left his position by the window, lowered himself carefully to the perch vacated by Brecher and slowly repeated his performance of fingering a cigarette from the packet to his mouth and lighting it without taking his eyes off Sullivan or letting his gunhand waver an inch. As he put the cigarettes back in his pocket, Sullivan called over to him, 'How about letting me have one of those?' and received, by way of reply, only a stare and a contemptuous grunt.

'Come on, Burgo—live dangerously. Light one and throw it to me.'

'Shut your mouth.'

'You know, Burgo, you have to be a pretty mean sort of a jerk not to let your prisoner have a smoke. I'll remember this when I come to see you in jail.'

'Don't make me laugh. You're not even going to get to see another sunrise.'

'Want to bet on it?'

Burgo drew on the cigarette and exhaled slowly. 'Not that it makes any difference,' he said, 'but I still can't figure you out.

135

If you weren't working for the Reds what was the idea of trying to wreck our little scheme for having them chucked out of Malta?'

'You really want to know?'

'Why not,' Burgo shrugged. 'It'll help kill the time till my colleagues get back here.'

'Well, let me start by asking *you* a question. Would you have done this thing in reverse—I mean if the Russians had offered you the same kind of money to frame up the Americans?'

'Maybe. But I like it a lot better this way.'

'Why, Burgo?'

'What do you mean, why? I'm against communism, that's why.'

'And *for* democracy?'

'Correct!'

Sullivan shook his head. 'You don't know what the word means, Burgo. Paul Spitari could tell you. He fought and won a democratic election from an honest-to-goodness neutralist platform. Soon as he got in he went ahead and did what he had pledged himself to do. Then you and your lot come along and for squalid personal gain try to frustrate the democratic processes. If you're a democrat, mate, the Mafia's the Salvation Army!'

'Are you telling me,' Burgo sneered, 'that that's the reason you stick your nose into this business—to uphold democracy?'

'That's right. Free press division. The exposure of any conspiracy to achieve by stealth and corruption what can't be achieved constitutionally.'

'You're boring me. I've a good mind to knock you off right now.' Burgo raised the gun from his knee and squinted along the barrel, and Sullivan tensed himself, riveting his eyes on the Maltese's trigger-finger. If he was going to have a go, it might just as well be now, before the other two arrived to lengthen the odds.

They were facing each other across the whitewashed room —rigid, tightlipped, graven images of coiled energy caught in the harsh light from the single bulb dangling from the ceiling—until the finger on the trigger loosened and Burgo's elbow slowly returned to rest on his thigh.

'What's stopping you, Burgo? Scared you'll miss?'

'You'll find out, soon enough. I don't want to waste you. There's still one last little service you're going to do for us—as a corpse, my friend.'

'Care to let me in on it. I promise not to noise it around.'

Burgo took a last draw on his cigarette, released the smoke through his nose in two narrow funnels, then flicked the glowing stub across the room to roll between Sullivan's feet.

'Have that one on me,' he grunted.

Sullivan stared down at the smoking butt. He could pretend to accept Burgo's largesse, bend over to pick it up and, from that position, go into a swift low dive at the Maltese. If Burgo missed with the first shot, he could take him before he got the second shot in. Ten yards . . . two seconds of time, maybe . . . He glanced upwards, straight into Burgo's tight grin.

'If you're thinking of having a go, don't let me stop you. I won't even shoot to kill—just to cripple you awhile.'

The gun was up but slack in his grasp—taunting. Sullivan put his foot over the dying cigarette, gave it a twist and leaned back against the wall. The sound of a passenger plane, losing height to land at Luqa Airport, filled the room for a while, causing Burgo to get up and back towards the window, ears pricked not to miss any other sounds blanketed by the aircraft's engines. It was probably the scheduled flight from Rome; or possibly a charter-flight, loaded with package-tour Scandinavians eager to practise their English on the native population—much as the British and Americans delighted in the incongruity of black men in Martinique rattling away in French *patois*. The sound of the plane died away. In a few minutes the passengers would be enjoying yolly yokes with the Maltese Customs inspectors before radiating from the airport to their various coastal hostelries. To Sullivan, under sentence of death in this remote farmhouse, it was as if the only ship on a barren horizon had steamed on past, blind to the signals from his desert island . . .

Burgo, from his position near the open window, heard the

137

approaching cars first, tilting his head back and stiffening, a few seconds before the car horn sent out one long blast as it descended the ridge road. He got up and backed away to one side of the window and into a position from which he could contain Sullivan and the kitchen dooway inside the same cone of vision. The first car braked in the driveway. Then the second. Doors were opened and slammed and approaching footsteps crunched the gravel. The first person through the kitchen doorway was Daria, dressed in a sleeveless white shirt-blouse and green corduroy mini-skirt. She paused for a second on the threshold, her eyes flicking from Burgo to Sullivan and back again, before moving on in, keeping over to the far wall in response to Burgo's gesturing arm. Brecher followed, closing the door behind him, leaning back against it and passing a shaking hand over his ashen face. The other hand supported his revolver as if it were a barely-tolerable burden.

Burgo said, 'Where's the Mazzi girl?'

'She didn't show up,' Daria answered. 'I waited ten minutes for her, then I drove past her house. There were *two* policemen outside on guard. So much for your precious Avanzo.'

'I see . . . You reckon it was he who let us down, do you?' Signalling to Brecher to concentrate on Sullivan, Burgo directed his full attention to the Israeli girl. 'Now why should he do a thing like that?'

Daria shrugged. 'Lost his nerve, perhaps.' She was meeting Burgo's unwavering eyes with her own cool and steady gaze. Without even a glance at Sullivan, she added, 'After all, we don't know whom our muckraking friend here talked to between leaving the Hypogeum and putting himself in your hands.'

'Correction!' Sullivan called out. 'He knows all right. Tell her, Burgo. Tell her about the message I got through to Paul Spitari.'

Daria had turned her head towards him and there was in her blue-grey eyes, suddenly, an expression somewhere between fear and despair. Sullivan looked her slowly up and down, putting into it all the contempt he could master. 'You were a good lay, sweetheart, I have to give you that. Pity all

138

that talent's going to be wasting away in Paola Prison over the next few years.'

'I think,' Burgo said slowly, 'he is bluffing about Spitari. I go along with George. Our hero here thought he could wrap it all up on his own, without having to share any of the glory. But he told us the truth about one thing, Beautiful . . .' The two of them were staring at each other again. '. . . Something he just couldn't invent. The Russian uniforms.'

There was a dead silence. Daria's face, in profile, hadn't changed expression, but the colour had drained from it and, even without the gritted menace overlaying Burgo's last words, Sullivan understood then that the fear and despair he had read in her eyes were that he had already betrayed her, and that in doing so he had in some yet unfathomable way cut his one remaining lifeline.

'You were told to destroy the uniforms that night. You told me next morning you had done so. Why did you lie?'

'Haven't you,' she replied after only a second's hesitation, 'ever said you've already taken care of something when what you should have said was you were *just about* to do it?'

'I'll ask the questions!' Burgo snapped. 'So you were just about to burn the uniforms. *Why didn't you?*'

'Believe it or not—I completely forgot.' She was looking away, back over her shoulder at Brecher, still leaning against the door, then at Sullivan, then at Burgo's gun, now pointing at her stomach from a distance of about six feet. *She's losing her cool,* Sullivan told himself. *That last retort wouldn't have convinced a child of ten. But what the hell is it all about? The uniforms . . . the lie—it could only be that—about the two policemen outside Lina Mazzi's house . . .*

Burgo said, 'Maybe I believe you, and maybe I don't. George?' He was calling over to Brecher, inviting his opinion.

'She's lying,' Brecher grunted, 'about the uniforms and about the Mazzi girl. I'm going out to check if we've been followed.'

'Stay where you are, George. We'll kill two birds with one stone—give her a chance to prove herself, and bring anyone who might have tailed her in here, running. Keep them both covered.'

He cocked his revolver, sprang the chamber and, without taking his eyes off Daria, began to remove the bullets one by one. When there were five of them in his hand, he clipped the chamber back, turned it to line the remaining bullet up for firing, and stepped closer to Daria.

'This man—' he jerked his head at Sullivan '—has got to die and normally it would make no difference which one of us pulls the trigger on him. But suddenly it does make a difference. If you've as much to lose as we have by leaving him alive—and I'm talking about the Red fleet staying on in Malta—you'll shoot this commie-lover through the head. But just in case you get any other ideas—' he slipped his free hand inside his jacket and whipped out a thin-bladed stiletto '—I'll stay right behind you while you do it. Now turn and face him.'

She was standing a bare six paces away from Sullivan, gun in hand. Burgo was immediately behind her, one hand on her shoulder, the other holding the knife-point to the side of her slim neck. Over to Sullivan's right, Brecher had taken a step away from the door, to a position from where he could put a bullet into Sullivan or Daria equally easily.

He weighed his chances swiftly as she raised the revolver until the barrel was pointing straight at his head. There was only one shot in the chamber and he would be able to dodge it, by split-second timing. But then Brecher would get him, and Burgo would finish him off with the knife.

He stared over the barrel, straight into her eyes.

IO

Had she been capable of killing him, her eyes would have told him, for he was aware that one human being could not take another's life in cold blood without either a momentary switching-off of all feeling—in which case the eyes went dead—or else a tell-tale flare of obscene excitement. In Daria Safad's face as they stared at each other over the barrel, Sullivan read only a despairing awareness of her vulnerability and the bleak fear born of it.

She lowered the gun slowly, closing her eyes and remaining motionless as Burgo took it from her and backed away. From his seat in the recess, watching Burgo reload the chamber, Sullivan could almost hear the man's mind spinning away at new permutations of logic, risk and reward.

Brecher said, 'Let's get out, fast.'

'Don't panic,' Burgo muttered. 'What do we do with these two?'

'Take them with us. They'll be cover for us as far as the bay, in case we were followed here. If it turns out we weren't, they can come with us on the boat. Part of the trip, anyway.'

'Just hold it a minute. You!—' he snapped at Daria— 'Get over there and sit down with your playmate.' He waited, scowling, as the Israeli girl walked forward to join Sullivan. Then:

'Who *is* she, George?'

'How do I know who she is? You brought her in, didn't you?'

'Only after she'd been fully checked out and cleared by—' He bit off the end of the sentence and Sullivan, clutching at a straw, took this to mean there was now a hope—however slender—he might be left alive. Why else should Burgo baulk at naming his paymaster?

Daria was sitting erect beside him, the hand nearest to him curled tightly over the edge of the stone seat, and as he moved his own hand over to cover hers, lightly, she turned her face to him with a nervous flicker of a smile and an answering clasp of his hand.

Burgo hadn't missed any of it. 'We're going to take a calculated risk. George,' he said, his eyes slowly raking the Israeli girl. 'If I'm right about it, it'll buy us time to relax and sort a few things out. If I'm wrong, it'll leave us no worse off than we are now.' He gestured to Daria with his gun. 'Get up and walk over to the window here!'

As she hesitated, her hand tightening around Sullivan's, Burgo cocked the trigger of his revolver.

'I'll give you three seconds—no more.'

Her hand slackened and she stood up, tugging down-wards at the hem of her mini-skirt. Burgo, from his stance over to the left of the far wall, kept his eyes flicking between the girl and Sullivan. Brecher was concentrating his gun and gaze on the Irishman and his will-power on staying erect—to judge from his own stance and appearance.

'Right,' Burgo grunted as Daria reached the window. 'Now you can lean through there and yell out "Help!" Just once. Loud as you like. Relax, George,' he added swiftly. 'I

142

was brought up on this farm. Nobody's going to hear her unless they're parked up there, watching the place.' He gestured to Daria, who was staring at him in disbelief. 'Go on—shout!'

She turned to the window, hesitated a moment, then leaned forward, thrusting the upper part of her body through the thick aperture. The action exposed the taut half-moons of her buttocks and the stretched wedge of nylon holding her crotch; and this was something else Burgo wasn't missing.

'*He-e-lp!*' Her cry—and it was the real thing, with all her lung-power behind it—seemed to be sucked into the enormous sound-vacuum outside and carried, spiralling, in all directions at once.

'That'll do!' Burgo snapped. And then, as she withdrew from the aperture, brushing the loose strands of hair from her face: 'Back up there against the wall!'

'Now what?' Brecher called over from the door.

'We wait for it. If she has any friends out there, this is when they have to show. If nothing happens, it means we're in the clear—for the rest of the night, anyway. We'll take it from there.'

Daria was looking across the room at Sullivan, and her face was composed but her eyes said, 'I'm sorry. There's no help for us outside.' Burgo must have caught the message, too, for he was now putting a cigarette to his lips and lighting it with an unhurried, almost complacent series of left-handed manipulations. The long minutes ticked away and Sullivan felt a compulsion to say something to the girl watching him from across the room, but he restrained himself. She would understand how he felt about his *gaffe* over the uniforms. Until he knew precisely where she stood in all this, he would serve her best by keeping his big mouth tightly shut.

'We're in the clear, George,' Burgo said, tossing his cigarette stub to the floor. 'Do you think you can manage to tie this one's hands behind her while I cover you?'

Brecher gave a grunt, moved slowly forward, then stopped, waiting for Burgo to set the stage. The bearded German seemed to have lost all personal initiative, as if withdrawn into a shell

143

of dolorous apathy, hoarding his mental and physical reserves against some final and crucial demand yet to be made on them.

'Move over here.' Burgo gestured Daria towards the middle of the room, narrowing the firing angle between herself and Sullivan, seated half-a-dozen paces beyond and to the right of her from where Burgo was standing. 'All right, George. Tuck the gun into your belt—at the back— and get up behind her. The slightest trouble from *you*,' he snarled at Daria, 'and *he* gets it first!' He waited until Brecher was standing behind the Israeli. Then:

'Take your shirt off!'

Her eyes flared 'What are you—?'

'Don't argue! Take it off and pass it to Brecher. We're short of rope around here.'

Sullivan said, 'You can have mine. It belongs to Georgie-boy, anyway.'

'Your gallantry's touching,' Burgo leered at him. 'But I'd rather have this bird's tits on view than yours. Get it off, sweetheart!'

She freed the shirt from the low waistband of her skirt and unbuttoned it down the front, clumsily, with trembling hands. There was a moment's hesitation, when it seemed to Sullivan she might be going to try something—a swift judo throw, maybe, on Brecher—and he tensed himself to move in the same second. The moment passed. She slipped the sleeveless garment from her shoulders into Brecher's waiting hands and quickly folded her arms over her naked bosom.

'Knot the shirt into a rope, George,' Burgo muttered. And, when Brecher had done so, 'Give him your wrists, Jew-girl. Nice and slowly, if you don't want to watch your boy-friend's balls being shot off.'

Watching her as she obeyed, bowing her head and rounding her shoulders to reduce the jut of her breasts, Sullivan wondered at the modesty of a girl who could be moved to shame and humiliation in a situation whose only remaining relevance was the issue of life or death. Then he switched his eyes to Burgo, and understood . . .

144

'Through there, George,' Burgo jerked his chin towards the door on Sullivan's left. 'Move around me, this side. There's a stairway leading down to a cellar. The key's in the door. Shove her in and lock her up.'

As Brecher prodded Daria forward at the point of his gun, Burgo circled around, putting himself between Sullivan and the door leading to the courtyard.

'Like to know the way it goes from here, man?' he said when they were alone.

Sullivan stayed silent. He was listening to the footsteps going down the interior passageway, hoping to judge the distance to the lower staircase.

'When George gets back to relieve me, I'm going down to that cellar and I am going to give that bitch a banging that'll rattle her teeth loose. You hear that, Sullivan? I'm going to pound that pot of hers into a steak tartare. After that, we're all going for a nice sea-trip.'

'Which only you and Brecher will complete—is that it?'

'That's about it ... I'm telling you this, Sullivan, because you're not all that thick. You must have worked it out for yourself that you and that Israeli bit, dead or disappeared in sinister circumstances, ought to just about cook Paul Spitari's goose for him. A Western journalist and an Israeli government official who between them had stacked up all the evidence needed against the Russian rapists—including their discarded uniforms—'

'You're out of your mind, Burgo. Spitari already has the real facts.'

'Correction! What he has is a *version* of them—at third hand. Wherever he turns for corroboration, he'll come up against a brick wall. Finally, the people will believe what they want to believe—you ought to know that.'

'What about the phony uniforms? They're not going to stand up to the simplest examination in any—'

'Phony, my ass!' Burgo cut in. 'They're the real McCoy. Do us the credit for not being that stupid!'

'And the imaginary Russian rapists just left them lying around, to be picked up by Daria Safad?'

145

Burgo was nodding his head, grinning. 'They dumped them, you see, after removing the identity-tags, to change into some civilian gear they nicked from a closed-up villa near the Jew girl's place. There was blood and semen all over their pants and it would have been a dead giveaway if they were picked up on shore, wearing them. Miss Safad obviously must have seen the Russians entering and leaving the villa, and went in after them to get the uniforms. Which was another good reason she had to be knocked off by the KGB.' He fell silent, staring thoughtfully at Sullivan, as if turning a new idea over in his mind. Then, as Brecher reappeared at the inner doorway:

'I know you can't be working with that Safad bitch. You would never have given her away about the uniforms, if you had been. Supposing I do a deal with you. Instead of giving her the treatment I just talked to you about, I'll put *you* in with her for half-an-hour or so. If you can persuade her to come clean about where she stands in this set-up, I'll let her off with a hole in the head, out at sea. You can tell her what the alternative's going to be.'

There wasn't the ghost of a reason why he should take Burgo's word on anything. All he would be doing, in getting the information from her, would be delaying for that time her ordeal at the hands of Alfonso Burgo. But up here he was in a pretty hopeless situation. Down there with Daria there was at least a faint chance of being able to work something between them.

He said, 'I won't promise her anything, Burgo, because I trust you just about as far as I could toss you. But I'd also like to know how she fits into this mess, so—' he shrugged his shoulders, 'if that's the way you'd like to play it—'

There was a dim light coming from a cobweb-festooned electric bulb high in the wall of the cellar. It illuminated a dank rectangular room, windowless and bare except for a huddle of rotting wine-casks at the far end and a pile of sacks against one of the walls. As the heavy door slammed behind Sullivan and the lock grated home, he called out, walking towards the casks, 'It's me, Daria. I'm quite alone.'

146

Her head appeared first over the top of the casks, her eyes wide, flaring like a trapped animal's out of her drawn face. She got to her feet awkwardly and moved sideways into view, presenting her back to him as he drew nearer.

'Please . . . my arms. They are going numb.'

Brecher had torn the shirt in half and bound one twist tightly above her elbows, the other around her wrists. And he had made a good job of it. While Sullivan worked on the knots, he said, 'We've got about half-an-hour. After that, their idea is to take us out to sea and—get rid of us. Give it to me straight, Daria. Are you expecting anyone to show up?'

'Not here.' She gave a little gasp of relief as her elbows were freed. 'I'm supposed to find some way of calling them to say where I am. It never occurred to me they'd find out —well—about the uniforms.'

'I don't suppose it did,' Sullivan muttered.

'I'm not blaming you. I—'

'Hold still . . . There! That feel better?'

'Thank you, Bob.' She turned slowly around, kneading her hands together, screening her breasts with her bent arms. Sullivan unbuttoned his shirt and slipped it off. 'Get into this. It'll help both of us to concentrate more efficiently.'

She had the shirt in her hands but was staring openmouthed at his shoulders and chest, at the purple bloodflecked weals scored by Maruka Faraclas's whip.

'*She* did that to you?'

'And more,' Sullivan grunted. 'But that's water under the bridge. No time for recriminations. Are you going to tell me who you are?'

She half-turned from him, averting her eyes while she curled her arms into the shirt-sleeves; and it was a measure of the gifts her body had heaped upon him less than twenty-four hours ago that his loins could stir now, in this bleak condemned cell, as he watched the liquid jounce of her profiled breasts before the garment enveloped them.

'I might as well tell you,' she said quietly. 'Whatever happens now, the secret is out. I work for the KGB.'

'But—well, for crying out loud, Daria, how the hell could you have— ?'

'Please, Bob!' Her hand was on his forearm, lightly. 'Let me tell it my way, from the beginning. And, Bob—' she looked past him, towards the pile of sacking against the bare wall '—I'm KGB, but I'm also a very frightened female at this moment. Could we sit down over there? And could I be close to you, with your arms around me, while we talk?'

Upstairs in the kitchen. Alfonso Burgo was watching George Brecher taking a swig at a flat half-bottle of brandy.

'Easy on that stuff, George,' he frowned. 'We've got a long way to go yet.'

'Just get me back to Athens, in one piece. I never want to see this goddam island again. Why the hell I ever—'

'Shut up and listen! I conned Sullivan into having himself locked up quietly so I can get over to St Paul's Bay and make the boat ready for a quick getaway. You'll be all right here for half-an-hour or so.' It was half-statement, half-question.

'Sure. But aren't you interested in Miss Safad's story?'

'It's obvious, isn't it? She came into this with all the right intentions, then went soft on us when it came to knocking off the Mazzi girl. All this stuff about her not showing up, and about the two cops on guard—that's just meant to scare us off the island, fast.'

'And what about the uniforms?'

'It's probably just like she said—she put it off and it went out of her mind.' He gave a snort. 'She'll be out of her mind all right, by the time I've finished with the bitch.'

'What are you going to do?' There was apathy in Brecher's voice and in every slack line of his body as he lolled on the upturned crate, head resting against the wall.

'When I get back, we'll bring Sullivan up here, knock him cold and tie him up. Then I'm going down to that cellar to screw the ass off the Jew-girl.' He flashed Brecher a lewd grin. 'Pity you're feeling under the weather at the moment, George. But you can grab your slice of her out at sea if you feel like it—before we dump them.'

'What's wrong with a couple of bullets in their heads here, and save ourselves a lot of time and trouble?'

'Everything. This old dump still belongs to me, for one thing; and it's there in the records. And we're not clear of the island yet. We might still need them as hostages. Make sense?'

'Go ahead,' Brecher sighed. 'I'm feeling too ill to argue with you. Get the boat ready and hurry back.'

'My real name is Nadia Kuznetsova. I was born in the Republic of Georgia, of Jewish parents, and educated like any normal young Soviet girl to believe in Marxism-Leninism, to reject all organised religion as the opiate of the people...' Her head was resting lightly against the ball of his shoulder, her hair a soft fragrant assertion teasing his cheek. He couldn't see her face; and he closed his eyes now to shut out the lithe symmetry of her thighs and the triangular shadow cast by the hem of her corrugated miniskirt. She glanced at the oblong, eye-level aperture cut in the heavy door of the cellar, then talked on in a lowered voice.

'My parents never tried to influence me about that. "One religion," my father used to say, "is enough for anyone. You have yours and we have ours. Let's leave it at that." '

'I became a member of the Komsomol when I finished school in nineteen-sixty-three and a year later started my studies in viniculture at the Agricultural Institute in Tbilisi. I was in my final year at the institute when the six-day war happened in Israel, and I remember being dismayed by the way two fellow-students of mine, both of Jewish parents, broke out in what seemed to me to be pure Israeli chauvinism— Zionism, if you like. Up till then, they had hardly ever mentioned the State of Israel in our discussions. Now, suddenly, Moshe Dayan was their hero and their only true homeland was the State of Israel. I couldn't understand how people could change their identity like that, overnight, as a result of one spectacular military victory. I mean, there are something like twenty-two separate ethnic groups integrated into the Union of Soviet Socialist Republics. What they all have in common is their Soviet citizenship, culture and patriotism, and

149

—I had always assumed, anyway—their overriding loyalty to the Soviet motherland.

'Last night, over dinner, I told you how I had pestered the Ministry of the Interior in Moscow until they gave me an exit visa for permanent emigration to Israel. Well, it's true I pestered them, but—let me tell you how it came about. It all started with a resolution I drafted in April, nineteen-sixty-eight for my delegation to a Komsomol congress in Moscow. In it we argued that the wisest way for the authorities to handle this Soviet-Zionist agitation would be to ship its leaders and militants off to Israel without delay, thereby letting the steam out of the movement. The resolution was carried. Next day, I was invited to dinner at the home of a high official of the Ministry of the Interior. There was a KGB colonel there and he seemed to take a great interest in my views and—well, to cut a long story short, instead of returning to work in Georgia I found myself being trained by the KGB for a special mission. When my training was completed, a year later, I was to start agitating at the OVIR offices for an exit visa to go to Israel. It would be refused. I would go on agitating, causing scenes, being arrested. Finally, they would grant me a visa, just to get rid of me.

'Well, that's exactly what happened. So I became an Israeli citizen, did my military service, and was not even required by the KGB to supply information about Israeli defences. They had something else planned for me and didn't want to risk jeopardising it. After my military service, I was to apply as a graduate in viniculture for a job with the Department of Agriculture. I would be put to work advising the wine-growers' cooperatives; but meantime I was to prepare, apparently on my own initiative, a paper for the department's export division—using data that would be passed to me by the KGB. This paper would analyse the prospects for expanding Israeli wine markets in the Western Mediterranean, with particular reference to Malta. Well, it worked out fine, and last year the department sent me here to promote its interests at the Malta Trade Fair. I must have done a good job, for they decided to set me up with an office in Valletta and give

150

me a small budget for promotion purposes.' She reached for Sullivan's hand and raised it to her lips. 'Now you know exactly how I got here, Bob.'

'All right. Now let's take it from there. How did you find out about the plot to frame-up the Soviet fleet?'

'We knew the CIA would be looking for some way to create antagonism between the Maltese and our sailors. And since their usual method in similar circumstances is to work through a well-rewarded local hireling, we kept a close watch on the contacts made by all US Embassy top people. Everything began to point to Alfonso Burgo as the one most likely to be doing their dirty work for them. So, a week before the Soviet ships were due here, I got to meet Burgo and it didn't take long to convince him I would accept any part he liked to offer me to help get the Soviet fleet banished from the island. I'm sure the fact that I was willing to work with him purely out of Israeli patriotism, without sharing in the pay-out, finally got me into the plot. Brecher and Faraclas were already here, standing by. And they had picked out Lina Mazzi as the best available pawn. They needed a non-Maltese girl to win her confidence, procure dates for her and all that—and that's where I came in. I was also used to distract the attention of some Soviet sailors who were having a swim out at Peter's Pool, while Burgo made off with their uniforms.'

Sullivan said, 'There's something I don't understand— but maybe I'm jumping the gun. When you found out what Burgo was planning to do, you obviously passed the information on to your KGB contact here. Why didn't the Soviet authorities nip the whole thing in the bud at that stage? Why let Burgo get away with it?'

'We decided to play for bigger stakes, Bob. We wanted to draw everyone involved in the plot out of cover—particularly Burgo's key contact in the CID, Detective Inspector Avanzo. We wanted this thing to happen just as Burgo had planned it—with me on the inside, assembling all the incriminating evidence. When the dossier was complete, I was to turn it over to the Soviet Embassy. We were quite sure what Paul Spitari's reaction would be, once the facts were established. The US fleet would be given its marching orders and told not to come back. Mission accomplished. Daria Safad vanishes into thin air. Nadia Kuznetsova reappears in Moscow, reporting for a new assignment.'

'Surely the whole case was wrapped up twenty-four hours ago? Why have you kept Spitari sitting on the hot seat?'

'We had decided to let Lina Mazzi make a fool of herself first, at the identification parades tomorrow. Only half of our ratings were on shore the night she was raped. It was a fifty-fifty chance she would pick out one or more sailors who couldn't possibly have committed the assault. We wanted her to do this before the Prime Minister knew anything at all about the conspiracy. However—' She paused, disengaged her hand from Sullivan's and raised it to pass the fingertips lightly over his wealed chest. 'There came a new turn of events. I told my people—and they agreed—that we couldn't wait any longer.' She fell silent again.

'The new turn being—?'

'From my point of view it was the fact, given to me by Burgo, that Brecher and Faraclas had you in their hands at the Hypogeum. From my comrades' point of view, it was the decision taken by Burgo to murder Lina Mazzi... I was told to wait until Burgo had returned to the villa to deliver the sleeping-drug and finalise the arrangements. I would report this to my contact and await instructions. While I was waiting, after Burgo had left, I discovered the uniforms had gone from the chest. Then there came the call from you, pretending to be Brecher. And a little while later Burgo called, telling me you had escaped from the Hypogeum. I made a rendezvous in Valletta with my contact and was given new instructions. I was to go and see the Prime Minister at once. I was to tell him I had allowed myself to become involved in the plot as an ordinary Israeli citizen, believing I was helping my country's cause. I was to say that they hadn't told me Lina was going to be raped—just, you know, molested and made rough sport of by the three men in Soviet uniforms. When I learnt what had actually happened I decided—according to this new version—to quit. But I was terrorised by Burgo into staying with the operation. Until they tried to get me to lure Lina Mazzi to her death. That's when I decided to make a clean breast of the whole thing to Paul Spitari and hope for clemency in return for telling him everything I knew.'

'How did it work out?'

'He listened to me and I think he believed my story. He showed me the uniforms your colleague had just brought to him a few minutes before I arrived at the Auberge d'Aragon, and I was able to confirm they were the clothes I had hidden in the villa. I told him that Burgo had now cancelled the plan for getting Lina Mazzi to my place, since he assumed you, Bob, had overheard our discussion. Instead, I was to drive her to a rendezvous near by the Kennedy Memorial. If it was clear I hadn't been followed by anybody, another car would then lead the way to a new hideout.

'The Prime Minister had already sent for the Commissioner of Police. They discussed what to do, in another room, and then gave me my instructions. I was to keep the rendezvous, but without Lina. I was to explain to Burgo that she hadn't turned up. As soon as I knew what his next move was going to be—and when it was safe for me to do so—I was to call the Commissioner and tell him where he could find Burgo and Brecher. Meantime, they would send a squad to watch the Villa Margarita from the time you suggested, but would make no move against Detective Avanzo, giving him a little more rope with which to hang himself.' Daria turned to stare up at Sullivan, her eyes troubled. 'It seemed a good enough plan, until I walked into that room upstairs and saw you there.'

'Sure, it was a good plan,' Sullivan grunted. 'And it would have worked—if I hadn't blown my mouth off about those uniforms.'

'You mustn't blame yourself for that, Bob. Why should you have had the slightest doubt I was everything I seemed to be?'

'Maybe I should have known when you tried so hard to persuade me—believing I was Brecher on the phone—to stop that Faraclas dike from having her kicks. There's no place for sentiment towards the enemy in your line of business.'

153

'And we're not enemies, are we, Bob?' It was a softly whispered appeal, uttered through trembling lips.

He turned his face away, tightening his jaws. 'I'll take up that point one of these days, assuming we get out of here alive.

11

Charlie Fenech and David Arrigo had checked the car-park of the Pescatore Restaurant in St Paul's Bay and were walking back to where they had left the Spitfire, on the main road out front.

'Where now, then?' Arrigo yawned. 'On up north—or back to civilisation?'

'I dunno. Let's spin a coin.'

They were standing by the car, with Fenech fumbling at his loose change, when Arrigo said quietly, 'Hold it, Charlie.' He was staring down the road, at a white Ford Anglia approaching from the Xemxija side of the great bay. 'Five-five—' he muttered as the car passed under a street lamp.

'Six-seven-five!' Fenech snapped. 'Let's go!'

There was still a fair amount of traffic filtering back from the sandy northern beaches towards 'civilisation' and in the time Arrigo took to reverse the Spitfire a taxi and two private

F

cars had got between him and the Ford Anglia. It would be impossible to pull around them until they cleared the narrow bottleneck of the old village of St Paul's; so, uttering a choice selection of mixed English and Maltese epithets, Arrigo hunched over the wheel, weaving out of line whenever he needed to keep the Anglia in sight.

'It's not Sullivan driving,' Fenech said. 'Looked like a Maltese chap.'

'What do you think we ought to do — flag him down when we get out of this bloody funeral procession and ask him where Sullivan is?'

Fenech uttered a negative grunt. 'We'd better play it cagier than that. The Editor wants to know what he's up to without letting on that we're watching him. We'll just stay put and see where this Joe ahead takes us.'

Clear of the village, Arrigo overtook two of the cars in front, leaving the Mercedes taxi between himself and his quarry. Two minutes later, the Anglia's rear direction-indicator started blinking out for a right-hand turn.

'The Bur Marrad road,' Fenech muttered. 'Let him get around the first bend before you go up after him. There's nowhere he can turn off before the Wardija crossroads. Do you think you can tail him from there on without your lights on, David?'

'With this moon tonight, I could tail a black Muslim around the blue Ridge Mountains of Virginia. You keep an eye on *his* lights while I look out for the potholes.'

They lost the Anglia once, on the tortuous road traversing the Wardija Ridge, but found it again as its lights suddenly came into view below the level at which they were travelling.

'Slow down a bit.' Fenech's head and shoulders were out of the window. 'He's swung off the road down there, into some kind of private driveway. It's probably as far as he's going.'

They reached the bend where the narrow dirt road forked down towards the old farmhouse, and parked the Spitfire a few yards further on, where the main road began to slope downwards. Fenech said, 'Stay at the wheel, in case he comes hareing out again. I'm going to take a look down that lane.'

Five minutes later he was back, opening the driver's door and motioning Arrigo to get out. 'It's an old abandoned farmhouse, just off to the left down the lane. The car's parked in the driveway with its lights out, next to a Cortina.'

'What do you want to do?'

'Nothing, till I've talked to the Editor. I'll take the car on into Zebbieh and make a call from there. You go and make yourself invisible, somewhere where you can keep an eye on the house. I ought to be back in about ten minutes.'

'Supposing they pull out of the place before you get back?'

'If Sullivan's with them—' Fenech slipped into the driving seat, turned on the ignition and put the gear-stick into second. 'Just give me one good hard shove, will you?'

'Here you go.' Arrigo put all his weight behind the windscreen pillar. 'You were saying—if Sullivan's with them?'

'Just trot along behind them,' Fenech grunted, 'scattering phosphorescent confetti as you go.'

John Carona was slumped in his chair, scowling at an untouched plate of ham sandwiches on his desk, when Fenech's call came in. The immediate cause of the scowl was the thought that he was missing the baked *timpana* pie his wife, Antoinette, always served up on Thursday nights. But the out-of-reach pie was in truth a surrogate irritation—a *pasta* scapegoat for the vexation caused by Paul Spitari's inaccessibility by telephone over the past hour and the brooding speculations this had promoted in Carona's ever-devious mind.

The Prime Minister was his friend. He was a regular guest, with his wife, at the Thursday *timpana* supper in the Carona residence at Pietá. After the meal, while the women talked clothes and children, Paul and John would sip brandy on the upstairs terrace, with its fine view over Msida Creek, and talk Maltese politics and world affairs until midnight, when Grace Spitari invariably intervened to 'move the adjournment'. There were few political confidences not shared by the two men; and after Antoinette had phoned to say the Spitaris were passing up her *timpana* that night owing to pressure of events at the Auberge d'Aragon, it was natural that Carona should immediately call the PM to find out what in fact was cooking in the political kitchen that night.

He had accepted the private secretary's regrets about being unable to bring the PM to the telephone at that time, and had let a quarter-of-an-hour go by before calling again. Same deal. Extremely sorry ... firm instructions not to be disturbed ... When a third call, half-an-hour later, bounced off the same brick wall, Carona blew his top and tongue-lashed the private secretary for failing in his clear duty, which was to pass a note, at least, to his master advising him that John Carona was on the line. The private secretary hotly protested that he had already done that thing, to no effect on standing orders; and Carona had to swallow the obvious fact that the cold-shoulder was political rather than personal—a protective device against giving him, as a newspaper editor, even a sniff of what was going on down at the Auberge d'Aragon that evening.

He at once dispatched a reporter and a photographer to Independence Square with instructions to stay put and to record and report back all comings-and-goings. Carona's instincts—supported by the respect he had for Sullivan as a newshound—now had him convinced there was a direct connection between the Irishman's evasiveness over the telephone earlier that evening and Paul Spitari's present inaccessibility. Something was breaking, and it had to be on the Lina Mazzi front. Recalling Sullivan's concern to get hold of Fred Fairchild, Carona summoned his night news-editor and the one remaining member of the night reporting staff and told them to get busy on the telephone, using every contact they had on the island to locate the young INB man.

They had just closed the Editor's door behind them when the call came in from Charlie Fenech.

'I'm in Zebbieh, John. We picked up Sullivan's car in St Paul's Bay and tailed it to this remote old farmhouse below the Wardija Ridge. David's keeping watch there right now. But it wasn't Sullivan driving.'

'Who the hell was it, then?'

'Some Maltese fellow. No one I know. There's another car

158

parked in front of the farmhouse. Very fishy atmosphere about the whole thing.'

'Nice work, Charlie. Hold it a minute while I think.' Carona snatched up one of the ham sandwiches, stared hard at it for a moment, then flung it across the room as it were a live coal. 'Where exactly is this place?'

'Well, it depends which way you're coming from. If you take the Bur Marrad road, up from the coast just past Salina Bay, then turn right at the Wardija crossroads—'

'Sod that! Listen—where exactly are you speaking from?'

'A place called Paul's Bar. Coming into Zebbieh from the south, it's the first turning on the left after you fork right into the village.'

'I've got that. Now, this is what you do, Charlie—stay put, right where you are. Don't budge. I'm getting onto the Commissioner of Police and there'll be a car-load of cops on its way to you in a couple of minutes. Lead 'em in and stay with 'em, Charlie. Get the story and hare right back here with it. Don't let anyone try to freeze you out. If they do, elbow right in again. I'll back you all the way, whatever happens. You got that?'

'Got it, John.'

'What's the number of that box?'

'Just a second . . . It's two-three-four-seven-nine-eight.'

'Stay put. The cavalry's on its way.'

Carona jiggled the telephone-rest and asked to be put through to the Commissioner's office in Floriana. He did not expect the police chief to be at his desk at that time of the evening, but there would be an adjutant on duty who would have the call transferred to the Commissioner, wherever he might be.

To his vast irritation, he was informed by the adjutant that the commissioner was in conference with the Prime Minister at the Auberge d'Aragon and could in no circumstances be disturbed.

'However, if you'd like to leave a message with me, Mr Carona, I'll see he gets it as soon as the conference is over.'

'That'll be too late,' Carona snapped. If he couldn't talk to

159

the Commissioner in person, he certainly wasn't going to get involved with an adjutant. By the time he had finished trying to explain to this desk-man why he wanted a car sent at once to the Wardija Ridge, the whole point of the operation might be lost. He knew now what he would have to do: he would have to by-pass the top brass and go straight to the one officer who would give him no argument once he had linked his request with the Lina Mazzi case.

'Be kind enough to reconnect me with the switchboard.' And, a few seconds later: 'This is John Carona of the *Malta Mail*. I want to speak urgently with Detective-Inspector Avanzo of the Criminal Investigation Department.'

Giuseppe Avanzo was Sicilian by birth and parentage, Maltese by nationality. In July, 1943, when he was barely five years old, his father—manager of a sulphur-mining company in Sommatino—was shot and killed by a local group of communists while resisting their takeover of the mine for a shortlived communist regime proclaimed after the Allied invasion of Southern Sicily. Two years after the end of the war in Europe, his widowed mother married a Maltese shipping agent based on Syracuse and, a year later, the family moved to Malta and made its permanent home on the island.

Giuseppe's two sisters made no fuss about adopting their stepfather's surname; but the young boy would have none of it. His father had died a hero's death, martyred by the communists. His name had been Avanzo. That was not only good enough for Giuseppe: it was a proud banner, a fiery torch he would hand on to his own sons. That way, the memory of a brave man would never be extinguished.

If Avanzo's childhood hatred of communism was a subjective and purely emotional thing, this was nourished rather than brought under scrutiny by the education and, later, by the intellectual climate of his adoptive island. Not for Malta, the dispassionate pragmatism with which its fellow-democracies to the north might judge the policies and behaviour of Lenin's legatees. There was good and there was evil in the world and they were painted shining white and sombre sinister black. The Church of Rome was an absolute good: the doctrines of communism an irremediable evil. There was no debate about this, any more than there could be a profitable debate about whether the *mistral* blew in from the north or from the south. But even had the island provided the opportunity and the data for an objective debate, this would have been a complete irrelevancy to Giuseppe Avanzo. The communists had murdered his father. He would be at war with them—all of them—until he drew his last breath.

It flowed from this that the American CIA—front-line fighters in the global war against Bolshevism—were Avanzo's spiritual brothers. Had he been approached, he would willingly have resigned from the police force, upon the neutralist Paul Spitari's election to office, and given his services to the CIA. It was Alfonso Burgo—no particular friend of his but one of his wife's cousins—who persuaded him he could play a decisive role in ousting the Soviet fleet from their Maltese haven and earn the gratitude of the CIA by collaborating with them from inside the force.

He hadn't liked the idea of a Maltese girl being gang-raped and had proposed, instead, that a victim be found from the ranks of the young British 'ravers' to be seen grooving away nightly at Sacha's Club in Paceville. But he had allowed himself to be persuaded that nothing less than a *Maltese* victim would spark the popular explosion, and he had accepted with inner relief Burgo's assurances that the Mazzi girl, far from being a maiden, had had 'more cocks up her than you and I've had haircuts'. Three more—however much uninvited—were neither here nor there . . . But when the cassette-recording of Sullivan's notes was played over to Avanzo by George Brecher and Burgo, and the Sicilian realised how Burgo had so effectively compromised him by insisting that he board *The Gurkha* in person to warn Peter Lund off the island, he blew his top. What the hell use was he to the CIA if this man Sullivan now had the power to put

161

him behind bars? Who was going to take care of his family while he rotted in Paola Prison?

They were sitting in an upstairs room at the Fort St Elmo end of Strait Street. It was Burgo's 'office'—a makeshift screening-room for the exhibition of 'blue' films to potential buyers. It was just past ten pm. Two miles away to the north-west, as the crow flew, Sullivan was paying his bill at the Tigullio before driving Daria Safad back to her villa. Burgo picked up the telephone and spoke to Maruka Faraclas.

'It's all set,' he said, gazing calmly across the table at the nail-chewing detective. 'When Sullivan calls you in the morning, after his night in the hay with our Israeli friend, you're to give him George's telephone number and then get across to George's place to work out the rest of the operation.'

The second call took a little longer. Without once addressing the person at the other end of the line by name, Burgo advised him that the converted motor-torpedo-boat, *The Gurkha,* was berthed that night either in Tripoli or Tunis with its owner, Peter Lund, on board, and that it was both urgent and vital that Captain Lund be regarded as a major security risk. Burgo listened in silence for a while before hanging up. He was smiling.

'You can relax, Giuseppe. Our friends are putting the matter in hand straightaway.'

About the time John Carona was getting the brush-off from the Auberge d'Aragon, Detective-Inspector Avanzo was alone in his office at CID headquarters, checking over the final arrangements for the next day's series of identification parades aboard the Soviet vessels. At the Soviet Commander's request, no uniformed police officers were to board his ships as escorts to Lina Mazzi or for the purpose of checking the crew manifests. It meant that a good part of the CID's limited force of plain-clothesmen would have to be deployed in Grand Harbour: and since the first parade was scheduled for 8.30 am Avanzo had sent most of the night men home and would be leaving only a sergeant and two constables on duty when he himself made tracks for bed.

The call came just as Avanzo was locking up his filing cabinet. One of the detective-constables put his head around the door.

'The Editor of the *Malta Mail* on my line, sir. Says he wants to speak to someone in authority and that it's very urgent.'

'Put him through on the extension,' Avanzo said, walking back to his desk.

In an island of a little more than 300,000 inhabitants, the great majority of whom were peasants, it would have been remarkable if two middle-class functionaries like Avanzo and Carona hadn't met each other a hundred times and been on first-name terms with each other. In fact, this was the case; but ever since Carona, as new Editor of the *Mail*, had swung the paper behind Spitari's battle for leadership inside the People's Party, a coolness had invaded the relationship between the two men. It was there now, in their opening exchange:

'Avanzo here. What can I do for you?'

'Ah . . . Giuseppe. This is John Carona. I take it you're in charge tonight?'

'You take it correctly.'

'Well, now listen carefully, Giuseppe, because there's absolutely no time to be lost. You're still masterminding the Lina Mazzi case, right?'

'Correct.' Avanzo turned to look through the open door of the duty room. The constable had replaced the receiver and was lighting up a cigarette.

'Heard of Bob Sullivan—reporting the Mazzi story for Intercontinental News Bureaux?'

'Can't say I have. There's a whole swarm of these fellows on the island right now.'

'This one's different. He's been digging a lot deeper than the others, and it looks like he may have bought himself some trouble.' Avanzo made no interjection as Carona drew breath, but the knuckles tightened in the hand holding the telephone to his ear. 'It's a pure hunch,' Carona went on, 'but two of my boys seem to have got onto some curious goings-on at an old farmhouse below the Wardija Ridge, and I'm pretty sure

Sullivan is involved. I would suggest you get some of your men out there straight away.'

'Is that all you can tell me about it?'

'That's all I know. Sullivan's disappeared and someone else just drove his car to the farmhouse. The boys tailed it from St Paul's Bay.'

'Who've you got on the job out there?'

'David Arrigo's watching the farmhouse. Charlie Fenech's waiting in Paul's Bar at Zebbieh, ready to lead the way in.'

'Very well, John,' Avanzo said. 'I'll attend to this personally. Thanks for getting on to us.'

'I want the story, Giuseppe—whatever it is. You can have the glory. All right?'

'I'll check into it. You can't expect me to say anything more than that.'

Avanzo hung up, walked across to the window and stood there, chewing his lip. He knew about the new rendezvous at the farmhouse. Burgo had called him from a telephone box on his way to St Paul's Bay, about three-quarters-of-an-hour back, to tell him they had been doublecrossed by Daria Safad and would be taking the Israeli girl and the Irishman on a one-way sea trip that night. Just listening to Burgo had caused a violent quickening of the stomach spasms Avanzo had been suffering from since learning of Sullivan's escape from the Hypogeum. All his instincts had started to warn him, then, that the plot was falling apart and that only a miracle would save him from professional disgrace, and worse. If Sullivan and the girl had now confessed—as Burgo had assured him—to being agents of the KGB, then their disposal on the high seas would not in itself give Avanzo any sleepless nights. On the contrary, the eliminating of Sullivan, following that of Peter Lund, now offered his best hope of avoiding personal exposure. But there had been so much bungling, right from the start; and now this—the sheer idiocy of driving about the island in Sullivan's hired car! Fortunately, neither John Carona nor his reporters seemed to realise exactly what they had stumbled upon. If he got over to the farmhouse fast, evading Fenech and Arrigo on the way, he might still be able to pull Burgo's chestnuts out of the fire without compromising his own position. He had a valid reason—his skeleton HQ staff—for going it alone. He knew the lay-out of the farmhouse, having looked it over with his wife quite recently. He would slip into it from the rear, tip them off about Arrigo and drive up, after they had nabbed the reporter—just in time to be locked up with Arrigo while Burgo made a getaway with his two prisoners.

Avanzo scooped up his jacket and strode briskly out of the office.

12

Sullivan uncurled his arm from around Daria and got to his feet at the muffled sound of a car door slamming somewhere up on the ground level. He went to the door and put his ear to the open grill.

'Burgo's back' he muttered, after listening intently for a while. Then, walking back and squatting beside the Russian girl: 'We've got to think fast. He told me, before he brought me down here, that if I could get you to tell the truth about yourself, he would let you off being—' Sullivan checked himself, frowning hard and looking away.

'Let me off what, Bob?'

'Oh, hell! Let you off being raped, before he does away with us both.'

'He has it the wrong way around. First he will have to do away with me.'

'He's an animal, Daria. A strong one. He'll manage it— without necessarily killing you.'

'So you think if you tell him all about me he'll keep his word?'

'Not for a second. But before he does what he plans to do anyway, he'll want to get me out of this cellar. And that'll mean leaving me upstairs with Brecher while he—'

'Go on, Bob.' Her voice was calm, her face attentive.

'I think I can jump Brecher, with Burgo heavily occupied down here. If you can fight him off long enough—' He paused again as the Russian girl's hand reached out for his. She said, 'Don't even think about whatever might be going on down here. If you succeed with Brecher, take my car and go for help. The key is under the driving seat.'

'Forget it! We're in this together now, all the way.'

'Burgo will have a gun. Please, Bob—!'

'So shall I, with any luck. And I shan't be sending Burgo a postcard saying I'm on my way down. Soon as you hear the slightest noise upstairs, you can start screaming your head off. If you can manage it, try to keep his back to that—' He broke off at the sound of footsteps on the stairway and rose quickly to his feet, motioning to Daria to stay put.

Burgo's face appeared on the other side of the aperture, dark eyes glinting as he took in the scene.

'Over against the far wall, Sullivan!' he barked. 'Hands in front! You!'—this at Daria— 'On your feet and face the wall, hands above your head!'

As they slowly took up their positions, the key grated in the lock and the door swung inwards. Burgo took a step forward, then a couple more to the side, leaving a clear passage out through the doorway.

'I didn't tell you could untie the bird, Sullivan. Or give her your shirt. Don't tell me she went all coy about flashing those tits of hers!'

Sullivan said nothing. He was thinking, *If the bastard gives me the smallest break, I'll jump him right here and take my chance on shooting it out with Brecher. That way the creep won't even get to lay his filthy hands on her.*

'Well, come on—did she talk or didn't she?'

'She talked.'

'Good. So she's saved herself from the old pork sword, at least. All right, Sullivan—you can tell me all about it upstairs.'

167

Affecting suspicion, he said, 'What's wrong with down here?'

'I want Brecher to hear it, too. Start walking,'—he jerked his gun towards the door—'nice and easy. And don't try to make a run for it. Brecher's waiting for us at the top of the steps.'

Burgo kept his distance, never taking his eyes off Sullivan as he stepped after him out of the cellar, locked the door, and followed him along the short passageway to the foot of the stone stairway.

'All right, George?' he called out. From the head of the stairway came an answering shout.

'Stand by, then! We're coming up!'

At the turn of the stairway, Sullivan looked up, straight into Brecher's downward-pointing gun barrel. The German backed slowly away towards the kitchen door, keeping a cautious space between himself and the advancing Irishman. As Sullivan passed over the threshold, Burgo's voice, closer behind him now, snapped, 'Slow down!' Then: 'Keep him covered, George, while I step around.'

Sullivan caught on to the guile in Burgo's command a fraction of a second too late—as the gun butt hit him and his head exploded into darkness.

From his perch on the empty crate, a pallid red-eyed George Brecher watched Burgo giving a couple of final tugs to the knots binding Sullivan's wrists and ankles.

'That ought to hold him, George,' Burgo grunted, getting to his feet. 'If he comes around before I'm finished down there, give him another clout on the head.'

'How long is this going to take you?' The German made no effort to keep the contempt out of his voice.

'Depends what kind of a fight she puts up, doesn't it? I wouldn't want it to be a pushover. She's got to be roughed up a bit first, for losing us that second pay-out.'

'You and Maruka Faraclas,' Brecher said '—you'd have made a great team. Well, go down and get it over with and let's get out of here.'

He couldn't see her through the paneless aperture in the cellar door, which meant she was either crouching behind the

168

casks at the far end of the room or else flat up against the wall one side or the other of the doorway. Baring his teeth, he unlocked the door and urged it a few inches inwards, keeping one eye level with the opening. The wall to the right of the door was clean. A quick sideways glance through the aperture—now at an angle with the other side of the wall—seemed to confirm she had chosen the barrels for her first stand. He was about to ease the door further open when another thought struck him, and he paused, narrowing his eyes. He could have just about put his head through the oblong aperture and peered downwards; but if she were crouching behind the door she could easily stick him in the eye from that position.

Tightening his grasp on the gun butt, he raised his right leg and gave the heavy door a sudden powerful kick. There came a cry, simultaneously with the crash of wood against an obstructing body, and as Burgo slipped quickly inside and locked the door behind him, Daria Safad pushed herself up from the floor a few paces away from him. There was blood trickling from the side of her brow, down over one cheekbone. She made to raise her right hand, to clear the dishevelled hair from her face, but checked the movement, wincing and clamping her left hand to the ball of the impacted shoulder. A short iron spike of the type used to pin wooden spars to sandstone walls lay at her feet. She glanced down at it—then, dazedly, at her grinning visitor.

He said, 'First trick to me, I think,' and, pocketing the door-key, advanced slowly towards her. She backed away, still clasping her shoulder, and then, as he made a dummy lunge at her with his free hand, spun around and fled for the cluster of rotting wine-barrels.

'That's is, sweetheart!' he called after her. 'Give me a good run for my money!' He picked up the spike, slipped it into one of the pockets of his jacket and, after clicking on the safety-catch, slipped the gun into the other pocket and started to peel off the coat. 'Come to think of it,' he went on, lowering the jacket to the floor and rolling the shirtsleeves high up his anthropoid arms, 'I often wondered what they meant by

169

having someone over a barrel. Now's as good a time to find out—what do you say, Jew-girl?'

She couldn't believe he was going to leave his jacket—and the gun—just where he had dropped it. But there he was, ambling towards her, long arms swinging clear of his body, his eyes and lips already relishing the obscene delights in store for him. When he was close enough for it, she sent one of the casks spinning at his legs and darted around him, heading for the jacket. And she reached it, and was fumbling for the gun as Burgo recovered his balance, whirled and came at her with the smooth speed of a wild pig breaking cover. Her hand was actually on the gun butt as he hit her—a jarring, openhanded blow to the side of the head that sent her sprawling. He hit her again as she scrambled to her feet with a vicious backhander across the mouth, and as she staggered back, gasping, Burgo's other hand snaked forward, fingers hooked, and ripped her shirtfront wide open.

For a little while they crouched, facing each other a few paces apart: the trembling, wild-eyed girl, blood flowing now from a split lower lip, and her leering persecutor; and against the ringing of her buffeted ear Daria was straining for that first sound from above and marshalling her lungs' strength for the screams that would drown it. But there was only Burgo's thick voice, taunting her.

'Come on, sweetheart—the fun's only just starting. Here—' he urged his face forward—'why don't you try scratching my eyes out?'

She started to back away again towards the casks, and he moved after her, talking to her as he went. He was telling her now, in his lust-sodden voice, what he was going to do to her in that cellar, spelling it out for her in terms of precise and clinical obscenity ... Her backward-groping hand brushed the belly of the nearest barrel and she darted around to put the breast-high barrier once again between herself and the chuckling Burgo. When he reached for the open rim, she made the error of thinking he was about to yank the obstacle away and took hold of her side of the rim in readiness for the deadly tug-o'-war. The next second she reeled back as the heavy wooden ribs came thrusting towards her, lost balance and let

170

out a sharp cry of pain as her damaged shoulder took the impact of the stone wall behind her. She was down on one knee and he was standing over her and slightly to one side, deliberately leaving an escape gap between himself and the next upright cask. She dived for it, was abruptly checked by his swift grasp on her shirt-tail, then wriggled and broke free, leaving the shirt behind. He was right after her as she went for the crumpled jacket again, and she swerved away towards the side, abandoning hope of reaching the gun and prepared, now, for a last-ditch stand with nails and teeth and her back to the wall. She whirled around to face him. He had come to a halt, halfway between his discarded jacket and the spot where the panting half-naked Russian girl stood at bay.

'I think it's time I started getting a bit rough with you, Safad,' he grunted as he unbuckled his belt, then unzipped his trousers and stepped out of them. 'See this?' He made a hard fist of his large right hand and brandished it at her. 'It's the knuckles for you, from here on.'

He came at her then, and she side-stepped a savage swing at her stomach, ran across the room and turned to face him again from the far wall. He took his time, following her. His object, she now realised, was to wear her down with running while he reserved his strength for the final assaults. There was still no sound from above. As she shot a despairing glance towards the door, Burgo closed in on her again, fists swinging.

'No use looking for help, sweetheart,' he grinned. 'Your boy-friend's out cold up there and trussed up like a boiling-fowl.'

She ducked a hook to the face and sprang away; but his foot shot out, tripping her and bringing her sprawling to the floor. As the first vicious kick drove the breath out of her lungs, an inner voice was screaming, *I mustn't faint! I mustn't faint!*

The Commissioner of Police stood framed in the doorway of the CID duty room. A uniformed inspector and a crash-helmeted sergeant of the motor-cycle corps were standing behind him in the corridor. Giuseppe Avanzo, who had been striding towards the door as it was flung open, came to attention and snapped his arm into a smart salute. Across the room, chairs scraped back as the CID sergeant and constables sprang to their feet.

'Just leaving, Avanzo?' the Commissioner inquired, pleasantly.

'Yes, sir.'

'For home?' The Commissioner's eyes were on the three men standing behind their desks.

'Eventually, sir. Just one call I—er—' His voice trailed off. There was nothing in this late-hour visit, or in the Commissioner's expression, to cause particular alarm, but Avanzo knew now, with a sickening certainty, that the game was up.

'Well, you'd better call your wife and tell her not to wait up for you,' the Commissioner said, otherwise ignoring the detective-inspector as he walked past him and on into the room. 'Because I'm putting you under arrest.'

Dumbstruck, Avanzo watched him as he conferred briefly with the sergeant, then snapped an instruction to one of the constables. The man sprang to the telephone and dialled a number.

'*Malta Mail*? The Commissioner of Police would like a word with Mr John Carona.'

The constable handed the receiver to the Commissioner and sidled away, staring in confusion from his sergeant to the rigid whitefaced Giuseppe Avanzo.

'Hallo, John . . . Yes, I'm sorry about that, but I've only just left him. John, I want to know about the call you just made to Inspector Avanzo . . .' The Commissioner listened in silence, brows contracting in concentration. Then: 'That'll do, John. Call your man and tell him we're on our way . . . Yes, I realise that and I'll talk to you about it later. Thanks a lot.'

Crouched behind a low stone wall overlooking the driveway, David Arrigo stubbed out the cigarette he had been puffing at and took a look at his wristwatch. Charlie Fenech had been gone a quarter-of-an-hour now, and if it hadn't been for the light slanting from that one window twenty yards or so away, it would have been reasonable to assume that the occupants of the farmhouse, whoever they were, were all now fast asleep. A few minutes after he had taken up his vigil, Arrigo had heard some brief indistinct snatches of human speech coming from the room with the light on. Since then: utter silence.

The mosquitos were giving him a bad time and the whole situation was becoming a bore. If he could only get close enough to take a peek through that paneless window, or at least through the keyhole of the door nearest to it, he might conceivably see something to give point to this bloody silly game the Editor had them playing at.

He had already made a peephole by working loose one of the uncemented stones making up the crude wall. Now he took another look through it, at the lay of the land. There was a risk to it, of course; but if he were to hop over the wall and make a silent run for that blank side of the farmhouse, he could take his time from there, creeping up to the corner and, if all was well, on to the closed door and the window beyond it. He stayed quite still for a moment, straining his ears for the sound of a car approaching from the direction of Zebbieh. The warm night around and above him brooded on in silence. 'Here we go, then,' he muttered, reaching for the top of the wall.

He made it to the blank side and waited there for a full minute before edging along towards the corner of the house. His heart was pounding and the palms of his hands had become moist, but he was enjoying himself. Treading gingerly over the fine gravel of the driveway, he reached the door and sank down until his eye was level with the huge keyhole. The key was obviously still in the lock: he could see nothing. He drew a deep breath and moved on towards the window. This was the tricky part. There was no way of taking a look into the room without exposing himself, and he was aware now, from the heavy breathing coming from somewhere inside, that the room was not empty. Well ... nothing ventured, nothing gained. He crouched below the window and then, inch by inch, raised his head above the thick stone sill.

Christ! There was a fellow lying on the bare floor, a few yards away from the window. He appeared to be tightly bound, hand and foot, and he was staring straight at David Arrigo! He had blue eyes and the naked upper half of his body was crisscrossed with dark weals, as if the poor bastard had been flogged, or something. As Arrigo gaped through the window, the man on the floor made signals to him with his eyes and chin, indicating a part of the room out of Arrigo's line of vision. Cautiously, he advanced his head and shoulders over the sill until he could see right into the room. There was a bearded fellow with a bandaged head asleep in a sitting position against the wall to the left of Arrigo. His chin rested on his chest. One hand cradled a gun in his lap.

Arrigo had never met Bob Sullivan, having been out on a story whenever the Irishman called in at the *Mail* office. He pointed at Sullivan now and mouthed his name, and the vigorous nod he got in return was all he needed. He didn't waste time trying the door; it was quicker and almost certainly less noisy to slip, seal-fashion, through the gap in the wall and down onto the floor. In a matter of seconds he was sawing through the cords around Sullivan's wrists and ankles with the small clasp-knife he always kept clipped to his keyring.

A grip on Arrigo's arm spoke Sullivan's silent thanks. Then, motioning to the young man to stay still, he crossed the room in a few swift strides, plucked the gun from Brecher's slack hand and stood back, covering the German as his head snapped up, mouth gaping to shout.

'Not a sound, Brecher!' Sullivan hissed. 'Stay right where you are!' Then, quickly over his shoulder: 'Who are you with, chum?'

'Arrigo—*Malta Mail*. The Editor's had us out looking for you.'

'Great! Come here and stand over this jerk, and if he so much as sneezes, kick him right in the mouth.'

'But what's happening? I mean, who is—?'

'No time for talk.' Sullivan was already halfway to the inner door, gliding noiselessly on his sneakers. 'Someone needs me downstairs.'

He heard Burgo's voice—low and hoarse with gloating— as he reached the cellar door. '... *Couple more sacks underneath, sweetheart ... that's fine. Now let's have those legs wide open, like the randy little whore you are, shall we?*' But there was

174

only Burgo's voice—not a sound from Daria. Sullivan's jaws set hard as he put his face to the open grille.

Daria Safad lay inert and completely naked on the stone floor, her hips raised by a bunched wad of sacks, her arms and legs spread wide like the limbs of a starfish. He caught a brief glimpse of her face, swollen and blood-spattered, before the kneeling Burgo's back blotted it out. Pushing the barrel of Brecher's gun through the aperture, Sullivan snarled: 'On your feet, Burgo!'

He rose, slowly. He was wearing only a shirt and it was ripped open at one shoulder. His underpants and trousers lay a pace away from him and, beyond that, his rumpled jacket.

'Turn very slowly around. And get this, Burgo—I'd like an excuse for blasting you, right here and now. I'm hoping you might oblige.'

Burgo came around to face him. The marks of Daria's nails were on his face and bull neck, and the lust was still with him—a short vivid eruption parting his shirt.

'Where's the key of this door?'

Burgo hesitated, then nodded towards his jacket.

'Walk over to it. Pick it up by the collar—finger and thumb only. Make one move for the pockets and you're dead.'

He was doing as he was told. But as he straightened up, dangling the jacket in front of him, his right hand remained screened by the garment. Sullivan squeezed the gun's trigger and Burgo froze as the bullet ricochetted off the floor a few inches from where he stood and thudded into one of the wine casks at the far end of the cellar.

'Get that other hand above your head, where I can see it. The next bullet's got your name on it! Towards me, now. Slow and easy.'

'*What's up?*' It was Arrigo, leaping down the stairway and coming to a halt a few paces behind Sullivan.

'Stand by and shut up! Now—you!' Sullivan aimed the gun at Burgo's chest as the Maltese stopped in front of the aperture. 'Turn around with the coat held behind you . . . Now back up a bit.' He raised the gun to Burgo's neck and, making room for Arrigo, snapped, 'Get your arm in there and lift that

175

jacket out . . . That's good . . . There's a big iron key in one of the pockets. Get it and put it in the lock.' He jabbed the barrel into Burgo's neck. 'You! Back over there to the middle of the room! . . . Hold it there! All right, Arrigo—open up!'

As they stepped into the cellar, Sullivan said, 'What about Brecher, up top?'

'He fainted, just before I heard the gun go off. I thought I'd better get down here to see what—'

'Save it!' Sullivan cut in. 'Get over to that girl. Lift her up, gently as you can, and carry her out of this hole.' Keeping Burgo closely covered, he moved further into the cellar to scoop up Daria's twisted panties and skirt while Arrigo gathered the girl up in his arms and made for the door.

He took a last look at Burgo after he had closed and locked the cellar door behind him and tucked the gun in his belt. The man's face was convulsed and he was shaking violently, as if on the brink of an epileptic fit. Sullivan called to him through the grille: 'You're a pretty poor specimen, Burgo. What happened—did the cat get at it one night, while your mother was out whoring?'

Burgo gave a roar and came for the door like a bull on rails; and Sullivan took pains to keep his neck visible through the aperture until the very second Burgo's long arm came flashing through.

He had him by the wrist with both hands, and he gave the arm a twist, as if he were an oarsman, 'feathering' his blade. Then he broke it across the wooden sill and left Burgo there, screaming.

Epilogue

'If you'll just wait in here, Mr Sullivan, till the doctor's finished his examination...' The Sister indicated the waiting room before rustling on through the swing doors into the hospital ward.

As Sullivan entered the room, a girl standing in front of the open window turned quickly and took a pace towards him.

'Doctor?' Her hair was long, sleek and honey-coloured and her eyes glowed greenly, with yellow sparkles. She was uncommonly attractive.

'Not me,' Sullivan smiled. 'I'm just visiting.'

'I'm sorry! I—' A helpless little shrug of her shoulders. An embarrassed grimace.

He said, flopping into a chair, 'No need to apologise. I've been taken for much worse,' and when she turned back to the window he took a routine glance at her hips and legs and thought, *Yes... oh, Yes...*

But his mind wasn't really in it. In a few minutes he would be sitting at Daria Safad's bedside, gazing into those blue-grey eyes and wondering how you said goodbye to a girl you were still half-in-love with. *'It's been great knowing you'? 'Don't forget, now—keep in touch?' 'Look, here's my address in London, if you should ever be there, spying for the KGB...'?*

Thirty-six hours had passed since he had carried Daria out of the farmhouse and into the Police Commisioner's car, and the greater part of that time had been spent writing-up his full story and dictating a long statement for the police. But he had found time to telephone the hospital twice and to organise the delivery of flowers and a bottle of champagne. He had also found time, after he had woken up that morning from six hours of velvet sleep, to dwell upon his feelings towards the Russian girl and to contemplate where they might lead him.

The Police Commissioner had given him the all-clear to leave Malta until Burgo, Brecher and Avanzo came up for trial, and Bill Topper was urging him to fly back to London that evening. This he would do. But not before he had talked to Daria and sounded out her own feelings towards him. Of one thing he was sure: the thought that this might be their last meeting was intolerably depressing. Did it have to be? Surely the issue was simplified rather than complicated by her involvement with the KGB, for it at least presented her with a clear-cut choice: to defect and, profiting from Paul Spitari's clemency, to join him in London as soon as the Maltese authorities had finished with her; or to return to the USSR and banish all thought of a future together with him. He believed he already knew, deep down, the road she would have to take; it was the sullen weight of this knowledge that dragged his steps now as he rose to the smiling summons of the ward-sister and made his way out of the waiting-room.

Daria's back was propped up against the pillows and there were screens on both sides of the bed, isolating her from the other patients in the casualty ward. She made as if to smile as he approached, then blinked at him ruefully, her fingertips touching the small patch of tape over her lower lip.

'Three stitches here, Bob. No jokes or funny stories—please.'

There was another, larger patch at the side of her brow,

and a huge violet bruise across one cheekbone. But this was not the damage that was keeping her in hospital. She was under observation—as the Sister had explained to Sullivan over the telephone—for any internal injuries caused by that last savage beating inflicted by Burgo before she lost consciousness.

He perched himself on the side of the bed and cupped one of her hands in his.

'What did the doctor have to say?'

'He was most complimentary about my abdominal musculature. Almost lyrical, in fact.'

'As well he might be,' Sullivan said gruffly. 'When can you get up?'

'This time tomorrow, if I've had a good night in between.' She moved her free hand over, to cover his. 'That nice Commissioner of Police was here for quite a while, yesterday evening. He told me—everything—' Her eyes were suddenly awash. 'Bob, what can I say that doesn't sound—trite?'

He said, 'I'll settle for a kiss.' And then . . . remembering . . . 'Or am I straining my credit?'

She gave him her unmarked cheek and he moved his lips across it, savouring the salt of a tear. 'I have to fly to London this afternoon,' he murmured, nuzzling her ear. 'How do you feel about joining me there?'

Her head remained still but her arms went around him, drawing him closer. 'I'm glad you asked me, Bob. I was hoping you would.' But there was no relief in it—only melancholy. He pressed on, as if insensitive to it.

'I'll have the pad stocked up with Israeli wine, of course. And we'll get you a job, translating the works of dissident Soviet novelists.'

She urged him gently away from her and gazed up at him bleakly, shaking her head. 'I can't come, Bob. You must know that.'

'I see . . . You mean you're afraid to? Or you just don't want to?'

'Neither. That is to say, the part of me that wants to—' she closed her eyes '—so very much—' It was a whisper, with the quality of a prayer, almost, about it.

'Go on, Daria . . .'

'The part of me that wants to will never win against that

179

other part of me—the part you can never influence, Bob. I could come to you, darling. They would probably even encourage me to go. But it would bring you only great trouble.'

'Supposing I said I'd take a chance on that?'

'You'd be saying it because you believed you might be able to change me. But you couldn't, Bob. The more you tried—what we have now, this moment—the sooner it would wither and die.'

'So we might just as well strangle it now and have done with it?' It was back, suddenly—all the bitterness and sense of betrayal that had engulfed him, two mornings ago, when he discovered the uniforms in the old chest. He had no right to feel this way; it was she who was being honest now, and making sense, and he who was off on a romantic hayride. But that—godammit!—was precisely where he wanted to be, with this girl and no other beside him; and she wasn't helping him to see any straighter, with that pale miserable face, those tears seeping through closed eyelids . . . There was something he had been prompted to ask her, down in that farmhouse cellar, but had decided to spare her at the time. He reached for it now, like a lifejacket.

'While we're on the subject of strangling—' He broke off, frowning, as Daria started to shake her head.

'*You* talk of strangling—I don't. I want to keep it alive, Bob—here.' She touched her breast.

'Well, leaving that aside for a moment—let me ask you something. It's about Lina Mazzi. You realised, of course, when you set it up for her to be gang-raped by those three German deckhands, that she might have been badly injured —disabled for life, even?'

'I suppose so,' she answered, looking down at her hands, which he had released and which now lay limply across the folded-back sheet.

'She had done you no harm.'

A single shake of Daria's head.

'Yet you felt no compunction about condemning that young girl to brutal multiple-rape—perhaps worse?'

She took her time answering him. When she at last raised

her eyes, they met his own levelly; and they were empty of guilt. 'There is a saying in English—"My country, right or wrong." It's as old as parliamentary democracy. I came to this island to protect and promote my country's interests, by whatever means might be open to me. Yes, Bob, I believe that certain means—however immoral by normal standards—can always be justified by a moral end, and that the highest interests of one's country *is* such an end.'

It was Walter Masters, all over again. He stood up. It wasn't going to be easy, but he wanted to keep the welling contempt out of his voice, and perhaps he succeeded. There was no real way of knowing, for the Russian girl closed her eyes as he began to speak and kept them closed when, after finishing, he turned and walked out of the ward.

'You've got it all screwed up, Daria. You've just made moral heroes out of every tyrant, from Stalin and Hitler to "Papa Doc" Duvallier, who ever set himself up as the State. And for every US president who deliberately closed his mind to the monstrous infamy of Vietnam. That thing you quoted— "My country, right or wrong"—has no nobility to it. It's nothing more than the cheap testament of a chauvinist. The parrot-cry of a moral coward. Do you realise what you're saying when you give me that? You're saying you've sold yourself out. You've swopped common humanity for the cynicism of a ruling elite. Well, Daria, you'll find enough companions to travel that road with you. I can't be one of them.'

Paul Spitari rose from his desk and walked around to greet Sullivan with a warm double-clasp of his hands.

'I'm sorry you're in such a hurry to leave us, my friend. I had in mind an evening of poetry-reading in my house up at Naxxar.'

'I got the tip-off about that, sir,' Sullivan grinned, '—just in time to book a seat on the next plane out.'

Spitari motioned him to a comfortable chair by the open window and took a seat facing him. The strain of the past week still showed itself in the darkened tissue beneath his eyes, but he was chuckling as he sat down, his iron-grey hair stirring in the breeze from the vast harbour below and beyond the window. 'You'll be back,' he murmured. 'Don't think you've escaped me and my muse.'

They were both gazing across the harbour towards the four Soviet naval vessels lying at their moorings. Sullivan said, 'I shan't be here for your press conference this evening, Prime Minister. I was wondering if you might give me a preview, as it were.'

'Six pm embargo?' Spitari stipulated, his eyes twinkling.

'Agreed.'

'Well—if anyone deserves to be privy to my intentions, you most certainly do, my friend.' He put his pipe in his mouth and struck a match. After it was drawing well:

'I am announcing I have advised the governments of the USA and the USSR that all naval units must be withdrawn from this island as from noon tomorrow and must not intrude into our territorial waters from now on.'

'What about Nato?'

'They have one month to close down their headquarters and withdraw all personnel. Malta is from now on a non-aligned, neutral country. Our facilities will be fully available to the merchant and tourist fleets of all countries, but not to the naval vessels of the two super-powers. We shall review, in due course, the position as it affects the navies of friendly nations within the Nato and Warsaw Pact blocs.'

'And the embassies—US and Russian?'

'They are welcome to remain, as in other neutralist states. We want to do business with the rest of the world. Peaceful business. We want to be able to stand on our own two feet—independent of hand-outs from other nations' military establishments. It's going to be hard going for a while. But with the reopening of the Suez Canal, we ought to be able to balance our books pretty soon. We must never again be dependent on other people's charity—or self-interest. Above all, we want to live in peace. That's something neither of the two super-powers seems to understand.'

The girl with the honeycoloured hair and green eyes was sitting at a table in the airport departure-lounge, reading a newspaper, when Sullivan strode in after saying goodbye to John Carona. She looked up, startled, as he pulled out a chair and sat down.

'Every airplane should have one,' he said.

Her eyes opened wider.

'A doctor, I mean. May I prescribe a glass of champagne for the flight?'

She was smiling now, and again he thought, *Oh yes . . .*

'I always,' she said, 'try to do what my doctor advises.'

While the waiter hurried back to the bar, Sullivan said, 'That enchanting accent—Swedish?'

'I'm sorry you guessed right.'

'Why so?'

'Because now you'll be planning to take me from London airport straight to your bed.'

'The thought never crossed my mind. Till now.'

'If I believed that, I should be absurdly—' She hesitated, pursing her pink lips.

'Naive?'

'That, certainly. And incredibly disappointed.'